Spring Fling

A Southern College Novella

By Meda White

Spring Fling
Copyright © 2014 Meda White

Editor: Andrea Grimm
Cover Artist: Kari Ayasha, Cover to Cover Designs

ISBN: 194128700X
ISBN-13: 978-1-941287-00-2

DEDICATION

To Mama Dear, for the gift of an active imagination and
every word of life you've spoken over me.
Love Always

ACKNOWLEDGMENTS

Special thanks to Rob Cummings and Theresa, who let me know this isn't an impossible dream. Thank you to my critique partner Christina Kirby, my chapter mates from Southern Magic, my family, and friends for your support and encouragement. Lastly, thanks to my Hubba-luv and real life hero. Without your love, I couldn't write love stories.

Chapter One

Kellyn Crenshaw got up from her poolside chaise lounge in a huff. It was the middle of a warm day during Spring Break of her senior year of college, and she should be buzzed and happy. Instead, she was sick of seeing her drunk best friend, Indi, being the center of male attention. Especially, since Indi had a boyfriend back in Georgia.

Kellyn was growing increasingly jealous of her friend. Not only because the boys described Indi's body as smokin' hot, but because Indi had dark hair and eyes and could turn a pretty shade of tawny when she sat in the sun. Whereas, Kellyn was a red head with green eyes. The only tan she could muster came from a can or a spray booth, but both had left her splotched, streaked, and stinky in the past, so she tried to accept her ghostly state of existence.

If she were honest, she'd always been a little jealous of Indi who was outgoing and made friends easily. Kellyn considered herself lucky to befriend Indi freshman year because she pulled Kellyn out of her shell and helped her meet a lot of people. They'd had a fun four years and this Spring Break was supposed to be their last hoorah.

Kellyn moved away from the crowd and onto the white sands of Panama City Beach, Florida to spray another layer of SPF 7000 onto her exposed skin. Indi had talked her into the black bikini, and while Kellyn thought it looked okay, it left too much skin to be burned by the sun's harmful rays.

"I'll get your back." Pace Samson approached with his hand out.

"Thanks." She passed the bottle to him and pulled her hair to the side. Her ponytail was sticking through the hole in her baseball cap, but it was so long it would get sprayed if she didn't move it.

She jumped when the cold spray hit her back, and Pace laughed at her. He loved to laugh and joke and could find humor in most situations. They had become sort of friends since Indi started dating his roommate and best friend, Cobie. But, Kellyn didn't care for the rate at which Pace went through women. He did it faster than some guys changed underwear. Some of her sorority sisters had been left brokenhearted by *Pace who leaves without a trace*.

Indi and Cobie had been dating since Winter Formal, so Kellyn was over at Cobie and Pace's apartment more often than she cared to admit. She didn't have anything better to do and the guys were entertaining. It was even a little funny the way Pace would thrust his hips in a lewd gesture and joke about his conquests. Kellyn promised herself she would never be one of them.

"Do you think I need some of this? I'm not getting too much sun, am I?" He held his hands out and did a slow turn for her.

He had all-American good looks—light brown hair, mischievous blue eyes, and muscles. Many of the fraternity boys had beer guts, but Pace carried a six pack out in front.

Kellyn tried to focus on his skin, instead of his muscles. "Your shoulders look a little pink."

"Hit me."

She smirked at the thought of smacking him upside the head, but instead pressed the nozzle of the sunscreen. The wind caught it and blew it back in her face. She coughed and made gagging noises, trying to get the taste out of her mouth.

"Are you all right?" He barely contained his laughter.

"Yeah." She pushed his back. "Turn this way." She managed to get it on his shoulders then.

"Rub it in."

"You don't have to; that's the point of the spray."

"I know, but sometimes it doesn't get evenly distributed. For all I know, you could be writing '*Player*' across my shoulders."

"I wish I would've thought of that. It could be a Public Service Announcement to warn the unsuspecting ladies, but I'm typically not that mean."

"You're pretty mean to me."

She put the can between her knees and reached

up to rub the SPF into his skin. "You deserve it. You have boyfriend potential, but your track record sucks. You treat girls like meat."

* * *

"You think I have potential?" Pace turned his head to look over his shoulder at her. He ignored the negative remarks and wished he could do something about the reputation he'd garnered in his four years at college.

Kellyn rolled her eyes, which was an expression she did often around him. Even when he made her laugh, she would still do it sometimes. She had a great laugh and was funny herself, but she was quiet about it.

"There you guys are." Indi stumbled up and wrapped an arm around each of them. "Here, Kellyn, take my picture with Pace."

Just to be mean, Pace bent Indi over in front of him and pulled her hair. He made his "O" face, and Kellyn tried not to laugh as she took the picture.

"You are so crass." Kellyn handed the phone to Indi. "I can't see the screen."

Indi passed the phone to Pace. "Now, do me and Kellyn."

"That's the wrong way to phrase your request, Indi," Kellyn said. "He might take it literally."

"Too late." Pace snapped the photo. "I'm here to serve. I can't see the screen either."

"Don't put any of me on Instagram, unless I approve them." Kellyn bent to retrieve her sunscreen. "If I look like a heifer, I don't want it to be documented for posterity."

"You look hot, Kellyn." Indi nearly fell over as

she gestured her hands in the shape of an hourglass. "Tell her, Pace."

Pace didn't want to tell her because he knew she wouldn't believe him, but it was true. She had the whole bust-to-waist-to-hips ratio thing going on.

He teased her instead. "You're a hothead, must be the hair."

"Love the bikini, Kel. There's not much material." Indi reached for Kellyn's top.

Kellyn backed up and crossed her arms over her chest before Indi exposed boobage. He'd like to see that, but he didn't want the rest of the beach crowd to also catch a glimpse.

"I'm in need of refreshment, ladies. Let's go." He helped Indi up the stairs and back to their poolside chairs before he went to get them another round.

When he returned with the drinks, he found Indi on his chair. "Move, woman, or I'll sit on you."

Indi slid down to the end of the chaise, and Pace took his seat, which he'd chosen because it was between two hot girls. He handed Kellyn her drink.

"What's this?" she asked.

"Sex on the beach. Try it. You'll like it." He wriggled his eyebrows at her.

She curled her lip and scrunched her nose before she sipped it. "It's too sweet, but it tastes better than sunscreen."

Indi chose that moment to lie on her stomach. She was still on his lounge chair, and he was treated to a direct view of Muffy McMufferson. Indi reached back and adjusted the thin scrap of material between her legs.

"Um, Indi, I know you're just trying to get comfortable, but from where I'm sitting, that doesn't look very nice." Kellyn sipped her drink.

"I don't care. I'm sleepy." Indi crossed her arms and laid her head on them.

Pace wanted to get out of the awkward position of having his best friend's girl sprawled on his lap, but his legs were pinned under Indi's.

"Kellyn Crenshaw, long time no see, beautiful."

"Oh my God, Josh. Hi." Kellyn stood and hugged a surfer-looking guy.

Pace didn't like the way the guy kept his arm around her.

"I'm here with Sammy and Pete," Josh said.

"No way, where are they?"

"Down on the beach, let's go for a walk. I know they'd love to see you, especially with you looking so fine."

"Shut up." She swatted at him and picked up her cutoff jean shorts. "Hey." Kellyn poked Indi's shoulder.

Indi lifted her head. "Sup?"

"This is my friend, Josh, from high school. His big brother used to buy us beer."

"And we used to ride around on the country roads and hang out of the sunroof…and make out from time to time."

Pace narrowed his eyes.

"You're Juicy Josh." Indi popped up off of the chair. "I've heard what a good kisser you are. Kellyn didn't tell me you were so cute."

"You think I'd make out with an ugly dude?" Kellyn picked up her beach bag. "I'm gonna go hang out with these guys for a while. I'll meet y'all back at the room later."

"I'm hungry and I need a nap," Indi said. "Pace, take me to McDonald's."

It was his turn to roll his eyes. Since his legs were free, he got to his feet and caught up with Kellyn. "I can't believe you'd abandon me like this. Aren't you afraid of what will happen to her in my care?"

"I'm more afraid of what will happen to you." Kellyn winked. "Make good choices." She flung her ponytail around and was gone.

He crossed his arms over his chest and imagined Juicy Josh getting swallowed by a big shark.

Chapter Two

Kellyn had fun catching up with her friends, but too much sun and booze began to tire her out. She needed to get back to the room to eat, shower, and nap before it was time to get ready for the nightlife.

The looks she got from Josh made her a little self-conscious. They'd never gone all the way in high school, but they'd come close. The thought occurred to Kellyn that she could have a little fling with her old make-out partner. Spring Break was the perfect time for a fling.

"Are y'all going out tonight?" Kellyn asked.

"Pete and I are," Sammy said. "But, baby boy here is whipped, and his woman back home said no bars at night—made him promise."

"Oh? Who's the lucky girl?" Kellyn asked.

"Not girl," Pete answered. "Woman, she's older than me and has a kid in middle school."

"She had him young," Josh said in his

woman's defense.

"That's cool." She'd misread his harmless flirting. "I gotta go, but maybe I'll see you two later." She pointed to Pete and Sammy.

At the condo, it was cool and quiet. Indi was asleep on the couch, but no one else was around. They were sharing the two bedroom condo, which slept six people with one of Pace's fraternity brothers and his girlfriend. That couple slept in one bedroom and Pace had the other, since Indi had volunteered her and Kellyn to sleep on the foldout sofa. Apparently, having Cobie back out of the trip at the last minute had messed with Indi's head.

It was good for Kellyn because if Cobie had come, she and Pace would be sharing the sofa bed, and that was not her idea of a good time.

Kellyn grabbed a bottle of water and a granola bar before she went to get cleaned up. It was still quiet when she was done, so she laid back in the recliner next to the sofa and tried to sleep. When she couldn't get comfortable, she went to Pace's room. She contemplated her decision for half a minute before she crawled under the covers and fell into a deep sleep.

Sometime after dark, she woke up and stretched, bumping into someone. She turned to see Pace sleeping beside her. He looked like an angel when he was asleep and not having bad dreams. She checked the time and rolled back over. Ten more minutes, she thought.

The next time she woke up was when Pace rolled on top of her. She was on her side, so it was particularly awkward.

"Wake up," he said. "We have to get our groove on."

"Who says that?" She squirmed. "I can't move, and I'm trying not to panic."

"Are you claustrophobic?" He didn't move from his position, but he lifted his weight with his arms.

"Little bit, my cousin used to lock me in the closet when I was young."

He moved off of her. "Gosh, I'm sorry. And, you think *I'm* a jerk?"

"He was a different kind of jerk. And you're starting to grow on me." She sat up in the bed.

"Really?" He tilted his head and gave her a grin that melted her heart. "Damn, your hair needs help, Red."

She tried to smooth it down. "Yeah, if I go to sleep with it wet, it gets a little crazy."

As it turned out, Kellyn didn't have to fool with it at all. Indi had her straightener on-hand and proceeded to put beach waves in Kellyn's hair. It took forever, but Kellyn had to admit she looked like a Hollywood Starlet when it was done.

"Move over, y'all," Pace said. "I've got to fix mine."

Pace's hair always looked as if he'd just rolled out of bed—kinda sexy like, but Kellyn knew better. The boy spent more time gelling and taming his locks than she did her own waist-length tresses. If one hair was out of place, he'd fuss like a girl— worse than a girl.

"Put it in a ponytail and let's go," Kellyn said after watching him fool with it for so long.

"It's not quite long enough. Look." Pace pulled the hair on his crown up into a bunch on the back of his head.

There was only an inch of hair poking straight out, and Kellyn contained her smile as his biceps bulged with the gesture.

"You look gorgeous, Pace." Indi added another layer to her smoky gray eyeliner.

"You're not half-bad yourself for a girl who's dating my roommate and best friend." Pace winked.

Kellyn rolled her eyes. "If you two would stop flirting and primping, we'd be at the club by now. It's gonna take us an hour to get down the strip."

Cruising the strip, the stretch of road which ran by all the hot spots, was a rite of passage for all Spring Breakers visiting PCB.

"I'm so bummed Cobie couldn't come." Indi closed the lipstick case and smacked her lips. "Oh well, I'll just have to make the most of it. Won't I, Pace?"

The look Indi shot Pace could have melted chocolate, but Kellyn chose to ignore it, like she had all day. She was starting to wonder if something more was going on with Indi and her boyfriend.

Indi had always been a flirt, but this was the first time she'd been out, away from Cobie, since they had started dating. Still, showing how much you miss your boyfriend by rubbing all over his best friend didn't sit well with Kellyn.

* * *

"I need you."

Kellyn's head snapped around to see Pace instead of the muscle bound, dark-skinned guy who'd been on her caboose as they heated up the dance floor.

"Get off me, you leech." She turned to face him and pushed against his hard chest.

"No, seriously." He placed his hand in the small of her back and pulled her so close his jeans grazed the zipper of her mini-skirt. "If you don't help me, Indi is going to molest me and ruin my friendship with Cobie."

Kellyn smirked. "You're not man enough to tell her you're not interested?"

He pulled her closer so nothing separated their bodies but a few millimeters of cotton. "I know who interests me…and it's not Indi."

* * *

Pace had been patient enough, waiting to let Kellyn know how much he wanted her. She was within reach. Heck, she was in his arms, but the look in her eye spoke of defiance and distrust.

"What's in it for me?" she asked.

The question surprised him because she was the type to help others and not ask for anything in return. He had to play it cool.

"Save a relationship and a friendship." He hoped to appeal to her loyal nature.

She put her arms around his neck. "So you want to pretend to have a fling with me to get Indi off your grill and salvage your friendship with Cobie?"

"Yep," Pace said, knowing that wasn't the whole truth.

She smirked. "You're a good dancer. I guess I could do worse. Some of the guys who have been grinding on me smell bad—BO and beer farts bad."

Pace's head fell back as he shook with laughter. "At least you know I've showered recently." At her nod, he put his mouth close to her ear. "Kellyn, you crack me up."

She gasped as he took her earlobe in his mouth. "Don't do that." She pushed away.

"If we don't sell this, it won't work."

"Yeah, but Indi knows you've never been my favorite person. She won't buy it if we suddenly start making out on the dance floor."

"Fair enough, Red. Let yourself be charmed by me."

"Why not? I've seen plenty of girls get sucked into your magnetic trap and become helpless against your wiles."

"If you fall, I'll let you down easy."

She narrowed her eyes. "Arrogant ass."

"Confidence is sexy."

"Cocky is nauseating." A big smile lit up her face as she held his gaze.

He could play verbal ping-pong with her all night and not grow tired. She was one of the few people in his life who called him on his crap. He was tired of girls with no depth. And since Cobie had started dating Indi, he could see the benefits of having someone to share your life with. Pace thought he might be ready to connect with someone on a deeper level.

They spent most of the night dancing. And while he felt like the middle of a Kellyn/Indi sandwich much of the time, he focused his affection at its intended target, Kellyn.

The fun came to an abrupt end after Indi got into a fight over the phone with Cobie. She clung to Pace and cried as Kellyn tried to make sense out of what was happening.

Kellyn ended the call to Cobie and opened the Instagram app on Indi's phone. "This is what he's pissed about."

Pace saw the picture of him bending Indi over, and he gritted his teeth. "Who posted that?"

"I did." Indi wiped her eyes. "I thought it was funny."

"Also, this one." Kellyn held up a picture that someone else had taken of Indi lying on the chaise with Pace. The angle made it look like they were joined at the crotch.

"Oh, God." Indi cried. "Who posted that?"

"Jessica Hart," Kellyn said.

"That bitch, I knew she had a thing for Cobie." Indi looked around. "I'm gonna kick her giant rear-end from here to Mexico."

Pace felt a pang of guilt because Jessica was probably trying to get back at him since he hadn't called her after that sex-filled night a few weeks before.

Indi started shooting Tequila and a few shots later, Pace and Kellyn carried her out of the bar and took her back to the condo.

"Put her in the recliner while I unfold the sofa and make it up." Kellyn started moving couch cushions.

"Don't," he said. "You can sleep with me. We'll just put her on the couch and cover her up."

"I…don't know about that. If she wakes up and

is still upset, it would be best if I was out here."

"She's not going to wake up. Did you see how much she drank?" He dumped Indi onto the sofa. "Grab that pillow and blanket."

After covering Indi, Pace took Kellyn's hand and pulled her to the bedroom.

"Do you think you should call Cobie?" she asked.

"Not at this hour. He needs time to calm down."

"I told him something that might not be entirely true, but I think it might help," she said.

"Did you tell him you're hooking up with me?" He wriggled his eyebrows.

"No, although if we're pretending, I suppose you could tell him when you talk to him. Tell him how madly in love with me you are."

"I *am* madly in love with you, Red." He pulled her into a hug.

She put her palms on his chest and pushed him away. "We don't have to pretend if no one is watching."

"It was worth a shot." He turned his palms up as he stepped back. "What did you tell Cobie?"

"That Indi pretended to be with you, so other guys wouldn't hit on her."

"Did he buy it?"

She shrugged and took her pajamas into the bathroom. When she exited, Pace admired her black shorts and tank-top and the way her shiny, copper hair hung in flowing waves down her back and over her shoulders. He determined then to see this through, even if she only saw him as a pretend fling.

Pace donned his usual sleep attire—cotton shorts, no shirt—and slid under the covers next to Kellyn. Shadows danced on the ceiling, created by the moonlight coming through the window and the plants outside on the balcony. Pace lifted his hands, crossed them, and made it appear a bird was in flight on the ceiling. Kellyn made what she called an alligator that chomped after his bird. He made his shape match hers and called it a shark, since they were at the beach. Then he made a shadow that looked like Batman's head.

Kellyn dropped her voice a few octaves and added some gravel to it. "I'm Batman."

"Sounds like Batman has a five pack a day habit."

She laughed and rolled into him. He took the opportunity to slip his arm under her and pull her to his chest. She didn't pull away, but stayed there laughing as they tried to make Batman sound like a superhero instead of a chain-smoking billionaire.

Just before he drifted off, with her pretty red head on his shoulder, he fist-pumped in his heart.

* * *

Pace awoke from a dead sleep when he felt Kellyn's arm snake around his waist and slip inside the front of his shorts. His body reacted immediately to the external stimulation, and he reached his arm behind him to grope her butt.

"Make me forget, Pace. Make me feel good."

He pulled Indi's hand out of his shorts and scrambled over Kellyn and off the bed.

"Ow." Kellyn sat up and turned on the lamp by the bed. "What's the big idea?"

She looked from Indi to Pace, and her eyes went below the belt. "Oh…that's the big idea. I'll leave you two alone."

Chapter Three

Kellyn's cheeks were hot. She tried to get out of bed, but Pace stopped her. She looked to where his hand rested on her shoulder.

"No, you were right earlier, Kellyn. I need to be straight with both of you."

"I'm up for a threesome." Indi tried to take her shirt off.

Kellyn grabbed her friend's hand. "Stop it."

"I'm not interested in you, Indi," Pace said. "You're my best friend's girl, but even if you weren't, I prefer red heads.

"Since when are you picky?" Indi pouted.

"I've had a crush on Kellyn for a while, and she's finally warming up to me."

"You like Kellyn?" Indi giggled. "I knew it. I told Cobie you two would make a cute couple. I'm so happy." She flung her arms around Kellyn, and they both fell backward on the bed.

Kellyn rolled her eyes at him and gave him a

thumbs-up sign with one of her trapped arms.

"Indi, get off of her. She doesn't like to be pinned down." Pace pulled Indi's arm.

Indi sat up. "How do you know that?"

"I told you I like her. I've been paying attention."

"Now that we have that cleared up," Kellyn said. "Go to sleep people."

"Can I sleep in here with you guys?" Indi asked, batting her long black eyelashes. "I'll behave, I promise." Her lip quivered. "I'm just so afraid Cobie is going to break up with me." She laid back on the pillow and whimpered.

Pace pulled back the covers and patted Kellyn's shoulder. "Scoot over."

She complied, and once he was lying beside her again, he whispered in her ear. "Don't put me next to her, please."

Kellyn was proud of him for taking a stand and touched by his words, even if they weren't entirely true. She reached down and took his hand, intertwining their fingers. Pace turned out the light after he pulled her hand to his lips and kissed the back of it. Kellyn's heart fluttered in her chest like a hummingbird trying to get sugar water...or like a moth to a bug zapper. She had to remind herself it was an act.

Indi began to snore, then talk in her sleep. The talk turned to moans, and it became evident she was having an erotic dream because she writhed and called Cobie's name. The covers flew back, and Pace pulled Kellyn up and led her to the couch.

He lay on his side with his back against the

cushions of the couch and pulled her down beside him. His arms were around her as if he were afraid she might fall off.

"I'm not holding you too tight, am I?" he asked.

"Um, no." Her mouth was dry.

After she got over the initial shock of being so close to him in such a tight space, she relaxed and realized it was cozy. It made her feel safe, which was something she never expected to feel with Pace.

When she was almost asleep, he whispered, "I wasn't lying when I told Indi I have a crush on you."

Kellyn didn't know what to say, so she pretended to be asleep, and before long, she was.

Something flashed and she thought it was lightning outside. She opened her eyes to see Indi taking pictures of her and Pace cuddled up on the sofa.

"Indi, stop it," Kellyn said in a loud whisper. "Are you trying to piss me off? Because that's the result your shenanigans are producing."

"I need you. I'm all alone and you pick this weekend to hook up with Pace? It's not fair. What about me?" She started crying again.

Kellyn knew Indi could be high-maintenance, but she'd never seen her act *this* needy. Indi had been there for Kellyn many times, so even though she was annoyed, Kellyn couldn't abandon her best friend when she was so obviously going through something.

She wiggled out from under Pace's arm.

"You okay?" he asked.

"Yeah, go back to sleep." Kellyn took Indi's arm and led her to Pace's bedroom.

She tried to console and encourage her friend, and when Indi fell back to sleep, Kellyn took Indi's phone. She checked the photos and planned to delete the ones of her and Pace sleeping, but when she saw them, there was one she loved. It was sweet. She texted it to herself, and then deleted it and the others from Indi's phone.

She scrolled through Indi's texts with Cobie. It didn't look good. He sounded like Juicy Josh's woman, telling Indi he didn't want her going out, he didn't want her to drink, and he didn't want her talking to any guys. Indi might as well have stayed home. It didn't seem fair since Cobie was supposed to be there and had changed his plans. Kellyn wanted to know the reason, but was afraid to ask.

She still hadn't gone back to sleep when the sky began to lighten. She opened the sliding glass door and stepped out onto the balcony. The air was cool, so she went in and grabbed the quilt off the end of the bed. With the blanket around her shoulders, she leaned against the rail and looked to the east. It'd been a long time since she'd seen a sunrise, and something about it seemed significant, like a new day was dawning, metaphorically.

* * *

The sunlight streaming in the window hit Pace in the eyes. He sat up and looked out to see an angel, complete with halo, standing in the morning light. With the rising sun silhouetting her, it gave an ethereal appearance of her hair being on fire.

21

He reached for his phone and took her photo. He took several, trying to capture the essence, but nothing was as beautiful as the real thing. He slid the door open and joined her on the balcony.

"Brrr." He rubbed his arms. "Share a blanket with your boyfriend?"

She turned and smiled at him. He still had his phone in his hand, so he lifted it and quickly took her picture. He got it just before she protested.

"Positively angelic."

"Working the charm bright and early this morning, I see."

He removed the blanket from her shoulders and wrapped it around his own before wrapping her up with him.

"How is it that you aren't taken?" he asked.

"Must be my winning personality."

"Be serious, when was the last time you dated someone?"

"Last fall."

"Who was it?"

"Mike Jacobs."

"The football player? That guy is huge. Isn't he like six-eight or something?"

She shrugged. "Yeah, something like that."

"I'm impressed."

"Why?"

"I don't know. Doesn't everyone want to date a football player?"

She looked up and over her shoulder at him. "Do you?"

"Ha-ha. How long did you date him? Why did you stop?"

"We went out for a couple of months, but I don't want to say why I stopped seeing him."

He put his hands on her shoulders and turned her, so he could see her face. "Did he do something to you?"

"No, he was an okay guy. It just didn't work out."

"It's a funny story actually." They both turned to see Indi standing in the doorway.

"Tell me," Pace said.

"No, don't," Kellyn objected.

"Ooh, it must be good. Red is blushing."

"It's not bad on you, Kellyn," Indi said. "Let me tell him."

Kellyn dropped her head into her hands, covering her face.

Pace lifted her chin. "I want to see you when I hear this story." He was smirking, but he couldn't help it.

"After they'd been going out for about four or five weeks, Kellyn went back to his apartment with him. Things started getting hot and heavy, and when she asked if he had a condom, he didn't. She asked if he would go get one, and he told her he was too drunk to drive, but she could go."

"Can you imagine?" Kellyn said. "Me? At a skanky convenience store in the middle of the night, shopping for condoms?"

Pace shook his head. "No. You're too much of a *good* girl."

Kellyn made the curled lip, scrunched-up face look Pace was starting to find endearing. He tapped the tip of her nose with his finger.

"But she did it," Indi said. "She was all worked up."

Kellyn rolled her eyes at Indi.

"What?" Indi put her hands out palms up. "You said you were."

"What happened next?" Pace asked.

"Apparently, college students are bad about shoplifting condoms," Indi continued, "so they had them behind the counter, next to the cigarettes."

"The clerk was a burly, biker dude," Kellyn said. "So I shuffled over to the counter to browse the selection, while trying to play it cool."

Pace shook with laughter. "Did he offer to help you with your decision?"

"No," Indi said. "Get this, they were sold out of all but one kind—Magnums."

"I knew that wasn't gonna work," Kellyn said. "So, I bought a pack of gum and drove my happy ass to the house."

"You're kidding," Pace said. "A guy the size of Jacobs? I figured he'd have to roll it up."

Kellyn pressed her lips together and shook her head no.

Indi was practically rolling with laughter. "Kellyn said it would've been like putting a Vienna sausage in a summer sausage casing."

Kellyn covered her face with both hands.

"I didn't realize you girls talked about such things. I'm shocked." Pace feigned offense.

He was glad Kellyn hadn't made it with the football player. He wondered how long the poor sap laid in bed waiting for her to come back before he realized she was gone for good.

"You wouldn't leave me like that and not come back, would you?" he asked her.

"You wouldn't make me responsible for the condoms, would you?"

"No, I wouldn't. I guess he deserved what he got…or didn't get in this case. Did he call again?"

"Nope." Kellyn shook her head.

"I told her he was probably ashamed," Indi said before she abruptly changed the subject. "I'm hungry."

Pace kept the blanket around him and Kellyn until they got inside where they dressed and made another trip to McDonald's. After they ate, they decided to go out on the beach for a little while since it was warming up.

While reaching in his bag for his swim trunks, Pace pushed the box of condoms aside before he stopped with a smile. He held the foil sleeve for a moment before he presented them to Kellyn. "I'm ready when you are, Red."

She narrowed her eyes at him. "Dream on, player."

"Hey, your words are hurtful. A man can change."

"Yeah, but I don't think I want to be the one you practice changing on. You could change back, and then what will I have?"

"Unforgettable sex." He tossed the rubbers back into his bag.

"Nice word choice," she said. "Just because it'd be unforgettable doesn't mean it'd be pleasurable."

"You're afraid I'll let you down? Don't worry,

Red, I'll take care of you." He tugged at a strand of her hair like a ridiculous boy in grade school pulling the hair of the girl he liked.

"Maybe we should try kissing first," she said.

"I thought I might get slapped."

"But you thought giving me half a box of condoms would be okay? What fantasy world are you living in, chief? Cart before the horse much?"

"It was stupid, but I just wanted you to know I'm prepared."

"I hope you're prepared for a letdown."

"Oh man, girlfriend is gonna make me beg."

She stood up a little straighter. "It feels good to have the power. I've got to change. We can continue this verbal tug-of-war out on the beach."

While Kellyn was in the bathroom getting dressed, Indi pounded on the door. It opened and closed, and Pace was sure he heard retching. He moved away because if he smelled it, he would lose his breakfast too.

Kellyn and Indi came out a few minutes later.

"I think I'll be okay once I'm out on the beach." Indi's hand rested on her stomach.

"Pace, would you take our towels and get us set up? I'll pack the cooler, and we'll be down in a minute." Kellyn nodded toward the door.

Indi sat at the table and put her head in her hands.

Pace whispered to Kellyn, "Is she okay?"

Kellyn shrugged as Indi said, "I'm never drinking again."

"Sure," Pace said. "I've made that promise to myself about a million times."

"Go on, get." Kellyn handed him a giant beach bag filled with towels, hats, sunscreen, hair-ties, and other various beach paraphernalia.

Once on the beach, Pace watched and waited for what seemed like forever for the ladies to join him. He hoped whatever Indi had wasn't contagious. As soon as he had the thought, he looked up and saw them. He positioned Kellyn in the middle, hoping her presence would prevent a repeat of the previous day's cavorting.

Indi plopped down on her towel and groaned. Kellyn removed her cover-up and Pace stared. He'd only thought she looked good in the black bikini, the turquoise one she was wearing did something for her the black never would. It set off her eyes, making them bluish-green like the waters of the Gulf of Mexico.

"What?" Kellyn asked, looking down at herself. "Is something hanging out?"

"No, everything's covered." He smirked. "That's your color; you look damn good."

"You're only saying that because you're my boyfriend."

"Yeah, and I'm trying to get lucky." He wriggled his eyebrows.

Chapter Four

Kellyn was trying not to take Pace's looks and words to heart. She had no doubt once he *got lucky* with her, he'd move on to the next sorority girl.

Kellyn was also worried about Indi. In the three and half years they'd known each other, she'd never seen Indi get sick from drinking too much. Kellyn tried to tell herself it was because Indi was also upset about Cobie.

"Y'all, I'm going inside to lay down," Indi said. "The sun hurts my eyes."

"Can I help you?" Kellyn asked from her position on her knees, holding the SPF spray bottle.

"No, I'm all right. I've got my phone. I'll text you if I need anything."

Kellyn watched her walk away. "I wonder if I should take her home?"

"You may have forgotten," Pace said, "but I drove us here. We can leave if you think it's best."

Kellyn sat back on her heels. "I don't know

what to do. I've never seen her like this. Have you spoken to Cobie?"

"Yeah, I texted him a picture of you and me together."

"What picture?"

"The one Indi took of us watching the sunrise." He passed her his phone.

It was a great picture of the both of them. She sent it to her phone and opened his Pandora app to the Alternative Rock station.

He took the sunscreen from her. "I'll spray you."

"What did Cobie say?"

"You don't want to know."

"Something uncouth, no doubt."

"Something about carpet and drapes? I didn't know what he meant."

"Un-huh." Kellyn cut her eyes at Pace. "Has he been talking to his old girlfriend?"

"How am I supposed to know?"

"Because you're his best friend and he tells you stuff. Why did he back out of the trip?" Kellyn asked.

"He told me his dad needed him to help with the spring planting."

"Would he tell you if he was going home to see his ex?"

"Not if he knew there was a chance I'd get drunk and run my mouth or make a move on Indi."

Pace rubbed the sunscreen on her shoulders. The rub turned into a massage. Her neck was stiff from playing musical beds the night before. She closed her eyes and let him knead her tight muscles.

"Lie down. I'll rub your back." His lips grazed her ear.

A chill pricked her skin. That was one of her sweet spots, but she'd be damned if she'd let him know it. Kellyn blinked. It felt too good and she couldn't go there.

"I'm good, thanks, boyfriend." She propped on her elbows and opened her e-reader.

She'd been reading a book called *Ex on the Beach.* The title seemed like it might be appropriate for Indi's situation. Before they headed home the next day, Indi might be the ex on the beach. Kellyn hoped not because her friend had been happy, and Cobie normally treated her very well.

"Hey," Pace said. "After we lay out for as long as your delicate skin can handle, do you want to ride go-carts?"

"I love go-carts. It sounds like fun, but I have to make sure Indi is okay. I don't think I should go too far if she's sick."

"You're a good friend."

"Thanks."

"I bet you'll be a good girlfriend."

She lowered her sunglasses and looked at him. "When did this stop being pretend?"

"When I decided I really like you, Kellyn."

She rolled her eyes, but because her sunglasses were back in place, she didn't think he'd seen it. "For Indi and Cobie's sake, I'll keep up this sham of a relationship."

Pace rolled onto his side and propped his head on his elbow. "What is so terrible about me?"

She turned to look at him. Her mama told her if

she didn't have anything nice to say, to keep her mouth shut. But truthfully, there were a lot of great things about Pace and one or two bad ones.

"You're not totally hopeless. You are very charming."

He grinned.

"But, you use that to take advantage of people, sometimes."

"Can I help it if girls are too dumb to figure out I'm a guy trying to get into their pants?"

"Pace, they know your reputation, but they all hope they'll be the one special person who'll make you change your wicked ways. Girls just want to be special to someone."

"You're special to me, Kellyn."

"I bet you say that to all the girls. You only like me because I'm a challenge. As soon as you get what you want, you'll think less of me like you do all of those girls who welcome you to Bootytown, hoping they'll be your last stop."

He flopped on to his back. "How do you know all of this? I don't even know it myself."

"Because I've been in a unique position to watch you work the past few months." Kellyn couldn't believe they were having a serious conversation.

"I don't know how to do it differently. You're the only one who's ever given me a hard time, the only one who's confronted me. I guess you've earned my respect."

The word Kellyn heard was "guess". He didn't say he respected her and that was significant in her mind.

"I don't know what you want from me, Pace. I'm not going to teach you to be better at your game of love 'em and leave 'em."

"I'm tired of that game. Haven't you been listening? I want you to be my girlfriend. It's not pretend."

Kellyn lay her forehead on her arms. She wanted to believe him, but she didn't. "How 'bout this, Pace?" She propped up. "How about we get to know each other and have some fun. I don't mean naked fun, but that could come later. Let's see what happens?"

"Can I still call you my girlfriend?"

She couldn't stop her smile. "Yeah."

* * *

When they were sure Indi was okay, they went to the closest go-cart track.

"I want to go to all the tracks," Pace said.

"Settle down, D-Pock. Broke college student on board."

"What did you call me?"

"D-pock…deep pockets. I can't afford all the go-cart tracks. I'll video while you enjoy them though."

"Don't be silly. My dad's a financial guru. I'm glad to take my girlfriend to all the go-cart tracks." He put his arm around her. "I can't fly solo. We can race. If I win, I get a kiss at sunset."

She'd grown up in the country driving go-carts and Pace was a city boy. "You're on, sucker."

"I *am* kind of a sucker—a lip sucker. You'll see at sunset."

Kellyn tried not to imagine that. She loved a

little lip sucking herself. It was a big turn-on, but she'd never tell Mr. Stick-your-wick-anywhere that little tidbit about herself either.

They spent the afternoon at the local go-cart tracks. There were five tracks total and after four, they each had two wins and tons of pictures. The final track at Hidden Lagoon would decide the kissing fate for the night. Kellyn wanted to win, and she wanted to lose. She pretended to pout when Pace won the last lap.

As she carried the McDonald's bag full of food for Indi up to the condo, her heart began to beat faster. She pretended to ignore Pace's smug expression and tried not to show how anxious she was becoming. She made a pit stop to brush her teeth and get ready for the fated kiss.

When she came out of the bathroom, she found Pace's bedroom door was closed and locked. "Do you think Indi is okay? Could she have slept all this time?"

"Let's step onto the balcony," he said. "We can check the sliding glass door to the bedroom…and it's almost sunset."

Kellyn started to protest and back out of the deal. But her dad had taught her people who made bets had to pay the price. When she reasoned it out, the price wasn't so steep. It was just one kiss.

Pace took her hand and led her out onto the balcony. It was windy, but warm, and the sun was getting low in the sky.

Kellyn tried to hide her smile as Pace slipped his arms around her and pulled her close to his chest. They were both facing the western horizon.

When the big ball of fire kissed the water, Kellyn took a deep breath. "That's beautiful."

"Not as beautiful as you." He turned her around and captured her lips.

She didn't protest, but met him stroke for stroke as his tongue explored her mouth. She sucked on his lower lip and smiled as he gasped. He pulled her closer, and she melted into the kiss.

"So, it's true then?"

It took a moment for Kellyn's brain to register there was a third party present for their sunset kiss. As she rejoined reality and opened her eyes, she was pleased to see Pace was still into it too.

"Boyfriend," she said around his lips. "We've got company."

Pace pulled back and blinked a few times. "Damn, you can kiss."

"Thanks." She batted her eyes. "Lots of practice with Juicy Josh."

He narrowed his eyes and pursed his lips before he turned to put his arm around her. "What can we do for you, Cobie?"

Kellyn hadn't realized the voice belonged to Cobie.

"I had to come see for myself that you weren't screwing my woman."

"No, I'm trying to screw this one."

It took all of Kellyn's restraint not to slap Pace. Her bubble burst—the one that had suggested she could be his special someone.

She pulled away from him. "Is Indi still sick?"

"Yeah, we need to talk," Cobie said. "Y'all come on in."

Indi was propped up in the bed with a rag on her head.

"Are you hungry?" Kellyn asked her. "We brought you food."

Indi's smile was weak. "Thank you. I'm glad you guys went out and had some fun."

"How do you know we had fun?" Kellyn asked.

"It's all over your face." She looked at Pace. "Both of your faces."

Kellyn turned to look at Pace, who grinned at her. Kellyn couldn't muster a real smile, knowing his was for show, but she turned the corners of her lips up in a semblance of the gesture.

"What's wrong with you, sweetie? Are you sick?" Kellyn climbed onto the bed and rested on her knees.

"You guys are our best friends," Cobie said. "So we need your confidence and help. Do we have it?"

Kellyn took Indi's hand. "Of course you have it. What's going on?"

"Pace," Cobie said. "I need to know we can trust you to keep your mouth shut for a little while."

"Because you are asking so nicely, Cobie, I give you my word."

"Good, because..." Cobie swallowed audibly.

"We're pregnant," Indi said.

Kellyn froze. It must be a joke, but Indi had been acting strangely—emotional, hungry all the time, craving fast food, and getting sick.

"A few weeks ago," Cobie said. "We had a little condom incident. So my advice is double coverage, if you're not in love and ready to commit your lives to each other."

"What are you going to do?" Kellyn asked Indi.

"I'm going to marry her, right after graduation," Cobie said. "She probably won't be showing much by then, and we need you guys to stand up for us."

Kellyn looked to Pace, whose back was against the wall and arms were crossed over his chest. He was shocked or stunned or both.

"I'll do whatever you need me to do," Kellyn said.

Pace cleared his throat. "Me too. But, have you considered? You know? Taking care—"

"Don't," Cobie interrupted him with a hand up. "Don't even go there. I'm Baptist and Indi is Catholic. We don't do abortion."

Kellyn dropped her eyes, wondering what she would do in the same situation. She wasn't much on religion or abortion. She knew what Pace would ask her to do, but she wasn't sure she could do it. Talk about losing respect for someone.

Kellyn stood by the foot of the bed. "I'm here for whatever either of you need." She went into the bathroom and closed the door.

Chapter Five

Pace knew he'd been insensitive, but he'd wanted to make sure his friend had explored his options. It seemed worse to be trapped into a fate not of your choosing.

When he thought more seriously about it, he supposed every time he had sex with someone, he ran the risk of knocking a girl up. He always practiced safe sex, but he'd never seriously considered the consequences. Or what he'd do if one of them came to him and said, "You're my baby daddy."

He needed to choose his partners more carefully. He already had when he'd picked Kellyn. He didn't think he'd marry her if he got her pregnant, but he'd offer to help financially, whatever she decided. The thought of raising a kid scared him to death, so he wasn't sure he could be hands-on, not at this stage in his life. He got the feeling Kellyn would want to keep it too, even if she didn't want him. On the other hand, she may think it would ruin her life.

Pace leaned against the bathroom door with Kellyn inside. "Hurry up, I've got to go."

"Go away, I'm taking care of business in here."

"Is that code for number two?"

"Get away from the door, Pace."

The water turned on in the bathtub, and he pounded the door. "Are you okay?"

"Go away."

He wasn't going anywhere. He slid down and leaned against the door. A half hour passed until she opened it, and he fell backward on the floor. She wore a towel on her head and one around her body. He could see up her towel, but he averted his eyes. She pressed it closer to her body, front and back, and took small steps to get around him.

Pace followed her to the living room, where Cobie had put his duffle bag and Kellyn's suitcase.

Pace sat on the arm of the couch. "Talk to me."

"If Indi is okay, can we go out tonight?"

"Yeah, but tell me what's on your mind."

She glanced at him. "Can I tell you later?"

"Yeah, I need to hop in the shower."

"Leave the door unlocked, and I'll come in and do my makeup in a minute."

"You don't need any makeup." He stroked her cheek.

She smiled the same weak-ass smile she'd given him before she went into the bathroom. "Thank you. You're sweet."

"Whatever you want, we'll do it." He started backing toward the bathroom.

She was upset and he desperately wanted her to open up and tell him why, when he should be running like hell.

"We'll see." With her towel still tight around her, she stepped into panties and hesitated when she caught him watching.

He swallowed hard before he turned to go.

Cold water was streaming over his head when he heard her come into the bathroom a few minutes later. When he was finished, he turned off the water and dried behind the curtain. He surprised himself because he'd been known to walk around his and Cobie's apartment completely naked, so the girls could see what they'd be getting with him. He was more of a summer sausage kind of guy.

More often than not, he had takers…more than one even. But, at the moment, it didn't seem important because he wanted to comfort Kellyn.

With the towel around his waist, he stepped from the shower and up to the counter. Their eyes met in the mirror, and she looked away.

"Kellyn, are you okay?" he asked as she combed out her wet hair.

She closed her eyes and nodded, but he knew she was lying. She plugged in the hair dryer, and he put the lid down on the toilet.

"Sit." He took the hair dryer from her and turned it on.

Taking his time, he used a wide tooth comb to pull through and dry sections of her hair. She sat with her head leaning forward and eyes closed. When he was finished, he turned the dryer off and set it on the counter.

"Take a look. I've never done that before." He put his hands on her shoulders and squeezed.

"Thank you for being so sweet, Pace. Let's go get drunk and *not* make a baby."

"Deal." He held his hand out and they shook.

When they left both of the other couples to go out, Kellyn wore a dark turquoise dress that showed a little cleavage and hugged every curve.

"I might have to beat somebody up," he said when they were in his SUV.

"Thank you, but you don't have to keep being so nice."

"I like being nice to you." He put his hand on his chest. "I live to make you smile."

"You're full of it." She grinned.

"There's a little one." He took her hand.

"I think it's a mistake," she said.

"What?"

"Them getting married. They're so immature. Yesterday, she was trying to sex you up, and he was telling her not to talk to any other guys after leaving her stranded to do Spring Break without him—the asshole. I give that marriage two years, tops."

"I know it's not ideal." He turned in his seat. "But Cobie is trying to do the right thing after an unfortunate accident. Some might see him as noble and the baby as destiny."

"I think he's been seeing his old girlfriend back home, and the only thing that got him down here was the possibility that Indi might be pregnant."

Pace couldn't deny it. Cobie had been home two of the last three weekends, like he used to do when he was dating what's her name. When he backed out of the beach trip, it was the first thing that had crossed Pace's mind.

"I don't know, Kellyn. I'm sorry you're upset. It bothers me too. There's nothing we can do about it but support our friends in whatever decisions they make. It's their lives."

"I know, sorry to be so cranky on what's supposed to be a fun party trip." She twisted her lips.

"You're always cranky."

"Thanks a lot. I retract my earlier comments on your sweetness." She tried not to smile.

"Let's go eat a bucket of shrimp and then get drunk."

She gave him a thumbs-up. "Shrimp and booze sounds good to me."

"How about a little *bumping uglies,* later?" He pounded his fists together once.

She shook her head. "I'd settle for another one of those hot kisses."

"So would I."

* * *

Kellyn had to tread carefully. She was in a mood thanks to Indi and Cobie, and Pace was offering her every comfort.

After a couple of beers and a belly full of shrimp, Pace helped her into his SUV, so they could join the slow crawl of cars on the strip to reach the club.

She leaned back in her seat. "You're a good boyfriend."

"I'm glad to hear it. Tell me how cute I am."

She turned to look at him. "I think you already

know."

"It's always nice to hear."

"Okay. You're cute. I think I like you a little bit." She held her thumb and forefinger about an inch apart.

"Is that all?"

"Well, maybe a little more. You're a good dancer, and I'll admit you can kiss. You're also a good friend to Cobie."

"I can be good to you too…if you let me."

"Stop smothering me." She fell over in her seat, laughing.

He shook his head. "I don't know why I like you, since you are so mean to me. You're nice to everyone else."

"Why *do* you like me, Pace?"

"Well…" He pursed his lips and looked upward. "You're not ugly."

"Wow! Sweet talker."

"You know you're pretty, Red. When you walk in a room, guys look twice, but there's more to you than good looks. You're funny and loyal. Let's see…you're honest, even when it hurts." He fake stabbed himself in the heart. "And you care more about others than you do yourself—"

"I'm not sure that's a good thing. Sometimes people treat me like I'm their doormat."

"You send them to me, and I'll set them straight. You've never let *me* walk all over you—another reason why I respect you."

There was that word again. He was pushing all the right buttons, and he didn't even know it. Maybe it was time to make him aware.

Pace put the car in park at the club, and Kellyn unhooked her seatbelt to give him a kiss that rivaled the sun in its heat. When she opened her eyes, she was in his lap, and she wanted him to take her back to the condo or crawl into the backseat.

"Kellyn." Pace was breathless.

"Let's go dance." She climbed out of his door, straightened her dress, which had somehow gotten severely twisted, and started for the club.

He took her hand when he caught up to her. He paid the cover and led her to the dance floor. All of the girls were staring, and Kellyn meant to prove Pace was taken, by her.

He spun her around and pulled her close. They danced, his hands on her hips, and hers around his neck. She'd never wanted anyone as much as she wanted him. He dipped her back and kissed her for all she was worth.

"I need a drink." She pulled him toward the bar.

"Hey man, she's hot," some guy said.

"I know." Pace wedged Kellyn up against the bar, so he could get their drinks.

Kellyn smiled at his possessive behavior. If she'd seen Cobie pull that with Indi, it would've made her mad, but having it done to her made her feel wanted and protected. Her skin tingled, and it took her a moment to recognize she was turned on. She wanted Pace and was ready to take those condoms he offered and put them to good use.

But they weren't going to be her only protection, she'd been on the pill since freshman year, but she never told the guys she dated. She was afraid they would be like Mike and shrug off the use of condoms. Pregnancy was only one of many things that sex could leave a girl with, and she planned to take every precaution.

Indi didn't take the pill because of her faith. Kellyn thought it was odd how people took some aspects of religion and left others; like premarital sex and contraception.

She wished the bartender would hurry; she was thinking too much.

Pace handed her a beer and toasted her. "To someone beautiful."

She couldn't help but wonder if he used that line on everyone. She smiled and sipped the beer. It didn't matter, a fling was a fling. She was going in with eyes wide open.

She emptied her cup. "Take me back to the room."

He set his half-empty glass on the bar and took her hand, leading her out. They made out in the parking lot for a little while before they left. She liked kissing him and sitting in his lap. She hadn't looked closely at the condoms he'd tried to give her that morning, but judging by her lap time, they must have been Magnums.

"Kellyn." He broke their feverish kiss. "We need to get back soon, or I'm gonna lose it."

She smiled triumphantly as she slid into the passenger's seat. "Does that happen to you often?"

"Never."

Once they got back to the condo, Pace took her hand and led her to the door. He touched her throat lightly.

"Your skin is so red. Did you get burnt?"

"The perils of dating a fair skinned girl. Friction burn looks a lot like sunburn, but goes away faster."

He ran a finger lightly along her jaw. "Does it hurt?"

She shook her head, and he gave her a quick kiss before he opened the door. Four sets of eyes stared at them.

"Hey, we're watching a movie. Get some popcorn and join us," Indi said.

She and Cobie and the other couple were seated four across on the couch, which left the two recliners for her and Pace. Kellyn let out a silent sigh of relief mixed with disappointment.

Chapter Six

Pace was oddly glad for the distraction. He didn't want to move too quickly with Kellyn for fear she might regret it. He made the popcorn and moved to the chair beside hers to share the bowl.

Before the movie was over, Kellyn was sound asleep. He remembered watching the sunrise with her. They'd both been up, playing all day. He made the sofa bed after the other couples went to their respective bedrooms and then squatted beside the recliner that held Kellyn. He slowly lowered the lever, but she opened her eyes.

"Time for bed, sleepyhead."

She smiled and nodded and let him help her the short distance to the sofa. She kicked off her shoes and slid under the covers, and he went to change into his shorts. Then he crawled into the world's most uncomfortable bed with the world's most comfortable woman. He took her hand in his before he drifted off to sleep.

Waking early, Pace found himself spooning her. In the past, when he'd woken up in the same position, he'd quickly found his pants and hit the door before the girl woke up. With Kellyn, he smiled and snuggled closer, closed his eyes and went back to sleep.

"Pace, man." Cobie shook his shoulder. "We're going to get breakfast. Y'all interested?"

Pace stretched, yawned, and rolled onto his back. "Kellyn, you hungry?"

She stretched too. "Not for McDonald's again."

"How 'bout the Awful Waffle?" Cobie asked.

"I'm there." Kellyn sat straight up. "Look, I'm already dressed."

"Talk about prepared." Pace chuckled as he got up to find his clothes. Her sense of humor was one of the many things about her he found attractive.

At the Waffle House, the foursome sat in a booth and placed their orders.

"I hope I don't get sick again," Indi said.

"Me too," Pace responded quickly. "Keep that pukey stuff away from me."

Indi ignored him and addressed Kellyn with a frown creasing her brow. "Do you think all the alcohol I drank will hurt the baby?"

"Um, I can't say for certain, but no. My mom didn't know she was pregnant with me until like four months. She drank and smoked pot until then."

"So that's what's wrong with you." Pace nudged her with his elbow.

"I'm really scared." Indi teared up.

Kellyn shot him a look, warning him to behave.

"Look," Pace said. "You guys are doing the

47

noble thing. My mother didn't love me enough to stick around, so your kid already has an advantage."

"So that's what's wrong with you," Kellyn said, but she wasn't laughing.

Pace shrugged. It was a sore subject, and one he rarely brought up.

"I'm sorry, Indi," Kellyn said. "We're making this about us when we should be supporting you. Tell us what you need and we'll do it."

"My dad is gonna kill Cobie." Indi cried.

Pace didn't know if he could stomach the drama surrounding this situation.

"We'll talk to him together," Cobie said, "after we talk to my folks. They'll be more supportive."

"Kellyn, will you be one of my bridesmaids? I want you to be my maid of honor, but my sisters will kick up a fuss if I pick someone over them."

"I'll do it as long as you don't make me wear pink. It's *not* my signature color."

"What about you, Pace?" Cobie asked. "Will you be my best man?"

"Dude, totally. I've never been a best man." The right words came out, but he squirmed in his seat. He admired Cobie's calmness and presence of mind. If he were in his friend's boots, he'd be flipping out…unless…if Kellyn were the one…hell, he'd still be flipping out.

"Um," Kellyn said. "I don't mean to be rude, but when did you two figure this out? I thought you were fighting and about to breakup."

"When she told me she was sick, it was the first thing I thought of. I haven't been able to get the condom incident out of my mind…and for good reason." Cobie squeezed Indi's hand.

"Are you sure getting married is the right thing to do?" Pace asked. "I don't mean to be a cynic, but I guess I'm jaded. Do you think marriage is the right move? Is it just for the baby? Or do you truly love each other?"

Cobie lifted Indi's left hand to show them the ring. "I bought this a month ago. I intended to propose after graduation."

"Even with old girl still calling you?" It was a low blow, but Pace had to call his friend out for everyone's sake.

The glares of Indi and Kellyn hit Cobie with ferocity.

"Yes, she's been calling…but I told her I'm in love with Indi."

"If you'd told her definitively, she wouldn't still be pursuing you." Kellyn practically spit the words out.

"You're right. I might have encouraged it at first. We have a long history, and it's nice to be wanted."

Pace didn't hear the rest because Cobie's words resonated with him. He wanted someone to want him—flaws and all. Kellyn had said girls want to be special to someone.

He looked over at her. She was watching Cobie with narrowed eyes.

"If you hurt her, I'll cut your giggleberries off and feed them to the bulls," she warned.

Pace instinctively covered himself. She wasn't one to mess with if you hurt someone she loved. He hoped to be counted among them some day.

* * *

Kellyn and Pace were free to enjoy their last day at the beach because Cobie had already taken Indi back to Georgia. They made a game out of collecting seashells.

On the drive back to school, Kellyn felt guilty. "Pace, I owe you an apology."

"Why's that?"

"I said something insensitive this morning. I'm sorry your mom left you. She was wrong because you're really special. She missed out by not knowing you."

He kept his eyes forward. "Thanks."

She shrugged and smiled. "I hope you're not mad." She searched for a new radio station. "Are you still planning to be my boyfriend when we get back?"

He cut his eyes over to her and made a funny face. "Are you crazy? I haven't hit that yet, so yeah, girlfriend. You're mine."

She pressed her fingertips to her forehead to stave off a headache. Pace's words reminded her of his track record. She liked being his friend, and she didn't want to be treated like the other girls. It would be best to cut and run, but they would finish school in ten short weeks, and she was toying with the idea of one last college liaison.

"What are your plans after graduation?" she asked.

"Well, my degree is in business with a specialty in finance. My dad has something lined up for me in Buckhead."

"That's so great. You might have missed out

on a mom, but it sounds like your dad's looking out for you."

"Yeah." He shifted his hand on the steering wheel. "What about you?"

"The same, I'm a money magician. I'm gonna steal your job and leave you in the unemployment line."

He cracked a smile. "Liar. You're gonna be a teacher."

"Yeah, both of my parents are educators, so I was destined for the field. I'm a double major, but I'll probably wind up teaching middle school English."

"Why middle school?"

"I don't want to deal with young kids who can't wipe themselves or punk high-schoolers. I remember those awkward middle school years. I still feel like that most of the time."

"I'm surprised," he said. "While I admit you're goofy at times, you don't seem awkward. You seem like you've got it all figured out."

Her throat got tight. "Thanks." She started twirling her hair until he captured her hand and held it.

"You don't have to feel awkward with me," he said. "I'm just as insecure. I just never let anyone see it."

"I hope the middle grade kids will like me. They'll probably think I'm totally weird."

"They'll love you." He lifted her hand to his mouth and kissed the back of it.

"Pace, what happens when we get back to school? With this?" She motioned her hand back and forth between them.

"I'll drop you off at your house and then go to my apartment and sleep for a few days. Then, I'll call you up and ask you to dinner. You'll say yes, and then," he started singing about getting drunk and screwing.

She laughed, even as she swatted at him. "Sounds like a plan."

She found Radio Margaritaville on XM and turned it up to drown him out.

* * *

Pace was glad it was just the two of them on the long drive home. He wanted to know everything about her, but she seemed to think she was too boring for him to care about. He had to pry information out of her, but he found her childhood stories endearing. They were both only children, so they connected while discussing the ways they entertained themselves.

When they got to the three bedroom house outside of town she shared with two roommates, he insisted on carrying her luggage up to her room for her. She had one of the upstairs bedrooms, across from Indi's. They shared a bathroom.

"Thank you." She set her beach bag on the bed.

He did the same with her small suitcase and then looked around the room. On her dresser was a picture of her with her parents. Her mom was attractive and thin. He'd learned from his dad to check out the mother before dating a woman if possible. There was a framed photo of Kellyn with Indi and another girl at a sorority function— probably pledge week or initiation.

"Did you catch hell during pledge week?" he asked.

"Not really. The worst thing that happened was Big Sister reveal night—that's Tessa in the picture—a couple of sisters drove us around and asked us trivia questions, and we had to do a shot for every question. By the end of the night, we were supposed to know who our big sister was."

"Did it work?"

"Sort of. The last thing I remember was falling off a deck. I woke up the next day with Tessa hovering over me."

"I got my ass paddled for my initiation."

"I know, I was there."

His jaw dropped. "You were? How embarrassing! That hurt like hell, especially since my big brother was the most muscled dude I'd ever seen up close. I think I teared up a little."

"You were just doing your duty." She winked.

"You have to admit the Greek system is something few understand who haven't lived it."

"I own that, but the best friends are made through adversity."

"We've kinda been through adversity the last few days." He closed the space between them.

"Yeah, we never really talked about it, but I think I already know how you feel." She looked down.

He stepped back. "You think I'm an asshole who would push for abortion if I was in Cobie's shoes."

"No, I've thought about it, and I think you're practical, especially after your mom abandoned you.

You'd take more time to consider your options, but in the end, you're decent, Pace. You'd help your girl in whatever way she needed. I think it would be just as hard for you to abort as it would for her."

"Why do you say that?"

"Because, although you pretend to be shallow, you're not." She took his hand.

No one had ever truly seen him before. He'd made a point to keep himself hidden. He moved closer to her and put a hand on the back of her head. "I've never let anyone in, Kellyn. Don't make me regret it."

"I'm not going anywhere, Pace…until graduation, and then I have to find a job." She grinned.

He stroked her cheek. "So, are we gonna do this Spring Fling thing until then?"

Her breath hitched. "Yeah."

He kissed her and tried not to think about the ten short weeks until graduation.

Chapter Seven

The buzz of her cell phone woke Kellyn. The display read, *Go look at the sunrise.*

She smiled and put on her Scooby-Doo slippers before she shuffled outside. Pace's Explorer was parked on her front lawn with the back open and him sitting there, waiting for her. Her headlights were shining, making it look like it was cooler outside than it was. She crossed her arms over her chest and went to sit beside him. He'd seen her in a tank top and sleep shorts, so she wasn't as modest as she might have been otherwise.

He handed her a to-go cup of coffee. It had just the right amount of cream and sugar.

"Thanks, boyfriend. You *have* been paying attention." She leaned her head on his shoulder and watched the sunrise.

"I don't miss much, except for sleeping without you last night. What's that about?"

She lifted her head to look at him. "I know. It

was weird, right?"

"You could've asked me to stay." He gave her a sheepish grin.

"You said you didn't want to rush this." She moved her coffee cup around in a circle. "We don't have a lot of time, but if you're afraid you're gonna hit it and quit it too soon, then you're right. We should wait."

He growled low in his throat. "I want to at least take you on a date first, but the braless wonder is making me rethink my good guy attitude."

Kellyn crossed her arms over her chest again as her face flamed. "Sorry. When you said go outside, I didn't think you'd be here. If I'd known, I'd have dressed."

"Then I'm glad you didn't know." He kissed the tip of her nose.

"You like surprising me, don't you?"

"I like seeing you smile. In fact, put that smile right here." He pointed to his lips.

"I have coffee breath."

"So do I."

She pressed her lips against his and didn't stop until she'd spilled her coffee on her bare leg.

"Whoa!" She jumped off the back of the Explorer and hit her head on the top window.

"Ow!" Her coffee hit the ground and splashed on her feet. "Dammit!"

Pace fell back laughing. "Those middle school kids are gonna love you, you klutz." Once he'd regained his composure, he sat his cup down and stood. "Are you okay, Red?"

He put his hands on her cheeks, and she forgot

her leg, head, and feet while she got lost in his eyes.

She swallowed before she spoke. "No more kissing while holding hot coffee. Lesson learned."

"You should go get cleaned up. I'll see you later." He gave her a quick kiss.

When he drove away, she was still standing, braless and obviously turned on, in her front yard like the lovesick school girl she was becoming. She shook her head at her own ridiculous behavior, another affirmation of her career choice.

* * *

Pace put on his cologne and stood back to look in the mirror. He admired his abs because he worked hard and avoided foods he loved in order to keep them defined. He flexed his pecs and hoped Kellyn appreciated his efforts. Other girls did, but that thought reminded him of Kellyn's lack of superficiality. She'd love a man for what was inside, even if the outside lacked appeal. He hoped she could see something inside him worth loving.

Anytime he thought of Kellyn and the L-word in the same train of thought, he stopped and slapped himself hard. He was *not* going to fall in love. It was a fling. When they graduated, it would be over.

He picked out a pair of white boxers with red lips all over them. Girls loved them. The thought immediately made him think Kellyn wouldn't find them cute at all. He put them down and picked up a pair that had Pinocchio on the front. Of course, the popular fairytale character had no nose and the fly was located in the middle of his face. He imagined Kellyn's laughter when she saw them.

Pace finished dressing and then texted Kellyn,

letting her know he was on the way. He couldn't remember the last time he'd been nervous about a date.

At her house, he took a deep breath before he knocked.

Kellyn opened the door and stood ready in jeans that hugged every curve below the waist, a loose green sequined tank top, and deliciously tall heels. His mouth went dry as she turned from the door to grab her purse. He tried to think of one of his usual lewd comments.

"Damn, girl, how did you get in those jeans?"

She turned to put a hand on her hip and tilted her head, narrowing her eyes at him. "You're asking the wrong question. You should be asking how to get me out of them. I hope those muscles of yours aren't just for looks because I'll definitely need your help."

In an instant, she put him at ease, and his expression changed from a sardonic grin into a genuine smile. "You look…" *hot, good enough to eat, all of the above*. He wanted to pay her a real compliment, so he filled in the blank with "beautiful."

He didn't think he'd ever told a woman she was beautiful and meant it, except his kindergarten teacher. He'd had a serious crush on Mrs. McKinney; she too was a red haired beauty. That memory made him think of all of the poor middle school boys who would be drooling over Kellyn in the future.

"Are you student teaching this semester?" he asked as he opened her car door.

"Yeah."

"What grade?" he asked when he was behind the wheel.

"Seventh."

"I bet you drive the boys crazy."

"Yeah, I look hot in my teacher clothes. Khakis and cardigan sweater sets are sexy. I almost wore that for you tonight, but I wanted to make it to dinner first, and you'd definitely rip my clothes off if I wore my school attire."

"I might've rip it off because of how hideous it looked. Cardigans? Please tell me you're joking."

"It's important to desexualize yourself in certain situations, but you'll probably never have to worry about that, being a man and all."

"I guess." He thought about what she was saying. He'd never considered that women had to be concerned about such things, but he could see it clearly now.

His dad's string of women had always exposed their physical assets. So had the college girls he'd dated. The other women in his life had been his grandmother, who was dead, and his teachers, all of whom were on the frumpy side. Some were actually frumpy, but the slimmer ones had only dressed to look that way.

"Is it weird having to dress one way for school and another for your private life?"

She shrugged. "It's kind of like changing for different occasions—one look for class, another for the gym, another for a date."

"Hmm. You have a way of explaining things, so I can understand them."

She patted his arm. "It's okay if you learn on a seventh grade level."

He laughed. "I was hoping you wouldn't figure that out so soon."

They spent dinner talking about their favorite movies and quoting the lines from them. He laughed at her *Nutty Professor* and *Major Payne* impersonations. She laughed at his *Forrest Gump* and *O' Brother Where Art Thou* voices.

On the drive back to her house, he said, "My face hurts from laughing so much."

"Mine too. Or it could be from chewing all that food. I might explode."

"You should watch your carbs. I know you have the metabolism of a twenty-two-year-old right now, but you don't want that catching up with you."

"Wow, I've never ever had to think about that before. Gosh, I don't know what I'd do if you weren't here to help me out, asshole. Watch your own friggin' carbs and leave me to mine."

"Sorry, God. I'm not calling you fat. I'm just sayin'."

"In the future, no comments about anything I eat, or you'll never get to see me naked."

* * *

Kellyn didn't mean to get riled up and start a fight, but as a girl who'd fought extra pounds since middle school and calculated every bite she took, she didn't need a hard ass man with twice her muscle mass and therefore twice her calorie burning ability, telling her what to do.

As her anger lost a little of its fire, she realized it would've been better to joke about it instead of take offense. Now, she was certainly going to think twice about taking her clothes off. Pace had no idea how hard it was for her to wear a bikini at the beach. Besides being the whitest girl alive, she was aware of her curves and her skin's ability to turn red at the slightest touch.

"I didn't mean—" Pace tried to say.

"I know, I'm sorry." She put her hand up. "You couldn't have known it was a sensitive issue for me."

"Tell me about it." He took her hand.

She told him, and to her surprise, he was sympathetic.

"My dad sent me to fat camp one summer," he admitted. "So, we have to make a deal; no fat jokes between us."

"Are you lying about fat camp to make me feel better?"

"No, I swear. Here, I'll call my dad." He hit a few buttons on his cell.

Kellyn protested, but Pace got his dad on speaker phone and asked him to explain it to her. Mr. Samson told her all about it and with a final note, said, "Keep my boy away from carbs."

"I think we'll have to help each other." Kellyn smiled at Pace.

"Do you call your dad on all your dates?" she asked when he'd disconnected.

"I never have," he said. "Most girls don't question what I tell them."

"That makes me sound like a real bit—"

"It makes you sensible. More girls should question what guys say to them. Half of what we say is to get what we want."

"Now, I'm gonna question everything you say." His honesty didn't put her at ease; in fact, it made her question everything he'd ever told her. "I'm gonna have to put your dad on my speed dial, so I can verify things."

He chuckled, but she couldn't laugh with him because a pain shot through her stomach. She placed her arm across her ribs to stem the burning pain as she suppressed a burp. A moment later, her stomach rumbled. She cut her eyes over to Pace to see if he heard.

His fist was pressed against his mouth as he too burped. "It's not as good the second time."

"Was that a throw up burp?" she asked.

"It had a little substance to it, yeah." He grimaced. "I hate to say it, Kellyn, but I don't think tonight's gonna be our night. I don't feel so good."

Chapter Eight

Pace drove as fast as he could to Kellyn's place. His butt cheeks were clinched as tightly as they could get to prevent leakage, but if he didn't get to a toilet soon, he was going to have serious problems.

"Oh God," she said with her hand on her chest. "I think I might puke."

"Um, how many bathrooms do you have?" He was trying for nonchalant.

"Two and a…," *burp*, "half."

He pulled into her driveway. "I'm gonna need to borrow the half, right now."

They both dashed for the house. Kellyn hit the stairs, and he ran into the half bath near the bottom of the stairs.

Explosive was not a strong enough adjective to describe his diarrhea. His stomach cramped as if his intestines were literally knotting up. It was so not the way he'd envisioned his date with Kellyn.

She was probably sick too, and he thought back to their meal. They'd eaten almost the same thing—steaks medium rare, baked potatoes, salads, and bread. Except, Kellyn ate extra bread, which was the source of his earlier comment. It was nice to know they shared a fear of carbohydrates.

He flushed the toilet, found a bottle of air freshener, and used it generously. By the time he washed his hands and reached for the doorknob, he had to go again. This time, he noticed Pinocchio had been sullied a bit in the seat. It was never a good thing for your girlfriend to find racing stripes in your boxers. He needed to get out of there as soon as possible.

His phone beeped and he read the text message.

What did we eat?

Probably the steak. I dunno, but this sucks.

It more than sucks, it stinks.

He laughed because she was right. *Gives new meaning to blow it out your ass. Sorry that I may have poisoned you on our first real date.*

Did you put the E-coli on our food?

Huh?

Never mind. I'm sorry too.

When he exited the bathroom, Kellyn was sitting at the top of the stairs. "Don't nobody go in there for—"

"Thirty or forty-five minutes," he finished her statement. "I love that movie too. It *is* Friday." He sat on the stair below her.

"I feel like Debo punched me in the stomach." She leaned forward with her arms wrapped around her abdomen.

"I'm so sorry. Is there anything I can do before…" He ran back into the bathroom and closed the door.

When he came out again, she asked, "Should we go to the hospital or something? I don't think I've ever had food poison—Oh God…" She ran into the bathroom between the upstairs bedrooms.

He climbed halfway up the stairs and sat down, knowing he should go home, but he wanted to be sure she was okay before he left her to suffer alone. He looked forward to a shower and a change of shorts.

When she hadn't come out after his next run to the downstairs bath, he knocked on the door.

"Get away from the door," she said, her voice strained.

"Can I get you anything?"

"A gun so I can shoot myself. This is agony."

"I'm coming in."

"No."

She was laying on the floor next to the toilet, spraying air freshener right at him. He fanned the air with the door and coughed until he started gagging. He kneeled and vomited in the bathtub.

When he thought he was done, he sat back on his heels and wiped his arm across his mouth. "I think I just shit myself while I was puking."

"Been there, done that." She still lay on the floor by the toilet.

"Should we call 911?"

She crawled over to the sink and opened the cabinet. Pulling out two washcloths, she wet them, squeezed them, and tossed him one, all while seated on the floor. She lay on her back and wiped her face with the cloth.

He wiped his face and then put the cool cloth on the back of his neck. He thought lying on the floor seemed like a good idea, so he did. The tile was cool, and since he had chills and was sweating at the same time, it felt both good and bad.

He closed his eyes, but opened them when he heard Kellyn ralphing. He got to his knees and turned on the tub to rinse his rag. He scooted over next to her and picked up her long hair that she was trying to keep out of the toilet, but had been unsuccessful. He put his cloth on the back of her neck and reached for a towel to try to get the puke out of her hair.

It wasn't until days later, he realized it hadn't made him sick.

He found more towels under the sink and turned on the shower. He stripped out of his clothes, folding them to conceal the damage, and climbed into the tub. Kellyn had strawberry shampoo and pomegranate body wash, which he used liberally. Something needed to improve his stench. He opened the shower curtain after he stepped out of the stream and wrapped his towel around his waist.

"Take off your clothes and put them outside the door, so I can put them in the wash. Get a shower, wash the puke out of your hair, and I'll be back to check on you in a minute."

"I have to hand wash this shirt," she said, pulling it over her head.

She was still sitting on the floor, wearing her

jeans and a lacy green and black bra. "There's a lingerie bag on the washer for the bra."

He almost asked her to explain, but with another stomach cramp, he dashed down the stairs. He might need another shower.

* * *

Kellyn hadn't been that sick in a long time. She wanted to call her mom, but as she leaned against the shower wall, she didn't think she had the energy.

When she made it to her bedroom, Pace was in her bed.

He lifted his head and let it fall onto the pillow. "Don't worry. I won't try to take advantage of you tonight. Don't think I could if I tried."

"That was a hell of a first date. I can't wait for the second." She opened her pajama drawer and realized there might not be a second date.

Pace had smelled her poop and seen her puke, neither contributed to increasing physical attraction.

"At least the bread didn't have time to stick to my ass," she added to change the subject.

"Talk about a weight loss plan," he said. "I think I lost ten pounds in your toilet."

She laughed as she slid her shorts under the towel and her tank top over the top. When she dropped the towel and turned toward the bed, Pace wasn't watching her anyway. He faced away from her in the fetal position, obviously still hurting.

"I'm gonna go see if Heather has Pepto," she said. "She has some stomach issues, so we might get lucky."

Kellyn went downstairs to the master bed and

bath her roommate Heather occupied. Heather had been in the house the longest, and lately, she spent more time at her boyfriend's apartment than she did at home.

Kellyn found the disgusting pink liquid and drank a big swig before recapping it, grabbing two bottles of water, and going back upstairs. The shower was on in her bathroom, so she put the water and Pepto on Pace's side of the bed before she slid between the sheets.

The next morning, she was tired and weak, and her mouth tasted like a cattle car. Pace was asleep, so she snuck to the bathroom and brushed her teeth. She found an unopened spare toothbrush and left it on the counter for him and went down to check the laundry, so he'd have something to wear home.

Kellyn was surprised to find her bra and sequined tank hanging on the line over the washer/dryer and their other clothes in the dryer. She folded the clothes and laughed at Pace's boxer shorts. They were adorable, and she imagined what they would look like on, with him creating the nose. She should be too weak to have dirty thoughts, but she wasn't. She shook her head at her own deprivation.

"Something funny?"

She turned to see Pace in the doorway of the laundry room, wearing a towel.

"Cute." She passed him the underwear.

She turned away to give him privacy, even though she'd seen him walk through his apartment in nothing but boots.

"These are definitely *not* my lucky drawers."

She turned to see him holding the towel and took a second to appreciate the boxers on him.

"I can see how they're not as sexy now as they might have been prior to…" he said.

"I don't know. You could get lucky in those. They might make you feel like a real boy."

"Only if I lie a lot."

"You better not." She gave him her serious teacher look. "How do you feel?"

"Like hell. How 'bout you?"

"Drained, but I think the worst is over."

"I'm glad. I hated seeing you sick." He leaned against the doorjamb.

"I hated being sick. I was going to thank you for dinner, but instead, I'll thank you for the thought."

"You're breaking up with me, aren't you?" He looked down and ran his hand through his hair.

"No, I'm trying to thank you, not only for poisoning me at dinner, but for sticking around to be sure I was okay."

"Oh." His expression was a mixture of relief and disbelief. "I'm sorry about dinner." He rubbed her arms with his strong hands. "We'll never go there again. Thanks for the toothbrush, by the way. Can I leave it here for later?"

The fact that he intended to return, made her day. "I'll put your name on it and tuck it away, so none of my other boyfriends use it to scratch their asses or anything."

One corner of his mouth tilted up. "I 'ppreciate you, Red. You know how to make a man feel special."

She batted her eyelashes. "I do what I can."

His lips landed on her forehead before he took his clothes into the half bath to dress. A forehead kiss was the kiss of death for a budding relationship.

"I'll text you later." He hugged her and walked out the door.

Kellyn felt like a helium balloon deflating with force. All of the hope and excitement she felt before the date, diminished after the door closed. If he texted her, there'd be a snowstorm in hell.

She trudged up the stairs and back to bed, wishing she had a roommate to talk to. It was the last Saturday of Spring Break. If she could do it over, she'd have ended it differently. She'd ruined her fling before it even started.

Chapter Nine

Pace opened the door of his apartment, hugged Kellyn, and planted a kiss on the top of her head, inhaling the scent of strawberries. He took the grocery bag from her. "That's a lot of saltines."

"It was buy one, get one free."

"Thanks, Kel. That's all I can keep down," Indi called from the couch. "Come sit with me. We're gonna watch a movie."

Kellyn assumed her usual position on the couch next to her friend. It had always been her go to spot because she didn't think anyone else would squeeze in. Pace was about to surprise her.

He and Cobie dished bowls of chicken soup and poured ginger ale. Cobie took his and Indi's dinner and Pace carried his and Kellyn's. He should've been afraid of the domesticity of the situation, but he wasn't.

The girls scooted, so they could all sit together

on the couch.

"Is this homemade?" Kellyn asked him.

"From scratch. One of my dad's girlfriends taught me how to make it when I was a kid. Kimberly, I think. Blonde bombshell, but they were all blonde bombshells."

Kellyn nodded as she blew on her spoon.

"Shh, stop talking." Cobie pressed play on the remote. "This is *What to Expect When You're Expecting*; we might learn something."

"Great." Kellyn rolled her eyes. "Research."

He loved that she did that. He could count on her eye-rolling after most things he said. But, she always wore a slight smile, like it shouldn't be funny, but it was. She understood his humor. She got him like no other girl ever had.

There was a point in the movie where a girl lost her baby, and with his arm around Kellyn, he could see her reaction. She looked at him with wide eyes and a hand on her chest. She feared the same for their friends.

Cobie paused the movie and interrupted the non-verbal comfort Pace gave Kellyn. "Just so you know, even if we lose this baby, I'm marrying Indi anyway. I love her, and I want her to be my wife."

"We know, Cobie." Pace answered. "You already had the ring."

When Cobie resumed the movie, Kellyn whispered in Pace's ear. "He was trying to decide who to propose to."

Pace had never said it out loud, but he felt the same way. If Cobie's old girlfriend had turned up pregnant, he would have done the noble thing and married her. He wondered how much Cobie was lying to himself about his situation.

Before he realized it, the idea repulsed him so much, he moved his arm from around Kellyn and stood. He had to get away.

* * *

Kellyn was concerned Pace might be sick again, but she was sure physical illness wasn't the problem. She wished she'd kept her mouth shut and she could accept Cobie's assertions that he loved Indi.

After ten minutes passed, she walked down the hall to the bathroom door and tapped lightly. "Are you okay? Can I get you anything?"

The door opened, and he pulled her inside before he closed and leaned against it. She'd been in that bathroom many times, but never with anyone, and now the walls were closing in.

He pulled her against his chest and hugged her with one arm. Her skin flamed from his touch, and her prior lethargy burned away.

"Sorry I deserted you," he said. "I know I'm supposed to be supportive, but I'm just really bothered. I shouldn't be. It has nothing to do with me."

"Except that it does. Cobie is your best friend, and you care about what happens to him. It's natural to want to protect the people you love when you see them making choices that may, or may not, be in their best interest."

"I don't want to think about them anymore. I just want…You. Here. Now." His hands lifted her by the waist onto the vanity.

He kissed her feverishly, and her rational mind tried to tell her to stop, but her body wasn't cooperating. The fire that lit low in her abdomen needed to be quenched.

His hands slid down her hips to her open knees, and he pulled them tight against his hips. He fit as though she were designed only for him, and her body responded with a volcano of desire on the verge of eruption. She was still fully dressed for goodness' sake, and some part of her logical brain was trying to figure out how she'd gone from zero to sixty in one hot kiss.

"Kellyn." Indi knocked at the door. "Are you guys okay? We heard…something."

Pace broke the kiss and staggered back while he took a deep breath and pressed his forehead against hers. Her body screamed for him to keep going, but her brain was regaining its dominance with the absence of his lips on hers.

"Pace, what's going on?" Cobie asked through the door. "We talked about this, man. Your bed is fifteen feet away. Don't do Kellyn like that."

Kellyn's face was on fire. "You talked about this? With Cobie?"

He moved away and pressed his back against the wall behind the door. Kellyn slid off of the counter, and when her feet hit the floor, she straightened her clothes.

"They talked to me about how I'm supposed to treat you. They don't want me to dick you over, pardon the pun."

Kellyn felt a bubble of laughter well up inside, and the more she tried to suppress it, the more it wanted to come out. She covered her mouth with her hands and walked into Pace's arms. As soon as she pressed the side of her face against his chest, it burst forth. She would've doubled over from it, but his arms held her close.

When her eyes found his face, she saw his smile and a glint in his eye.

"Do you want to spend the night with me, Kellyn?"

"We've spent too many nights together. Less talk, more action." Her lips found his, and in a flash, she was back on the vanity.

Another knock at the door, and Kellyn broke the kiss. "Get away from the door. If I have to come out there, my hair will be on fire."

"Oh hell, come on, Cobie," Indi said.

It was Pace's turn to laugh. "I bet that is a sight to see."

He loosened her hair from the low ponytail and ran his fingers through it a few times. It was a tender thing for him to do, and she felt a different heat in that moment. It started at the center of her chest and spread everywhere.

He placed his hands on both sides of her face. "Come on, beautiful, let's do this right."

* * *

Pace tried to calm his racing heart as he took Kellyn's hand and led her down the hall to his bedroom. She glanced around and went to the dresser to look at the photographs. She picked up the five by seven frame and turned to him, her gaze traveling back and forth between him and the picture.

Pace locked the door before he moved beside her. "That's my dad."

"You have his chin." When he smiled, she added, "And his lips. Very handsome."

She turned back to set the frame on the dresser and picked up the one beside it. In the picture, Pace was seventeen, and his grandmother was a young looking sixty-five.

"You were a scrawny teenager," she said. "I'm thinking your dad lied to me about the weight thing."

"We didn't lie. That was after a growth spurt, six inches in a year."

"And the woman?"

He explained how his grandmother had been the only mother figure he'd known, but she'd lived in Texas, so he hadn't gotten to see her often. "She died shortly after that picture was taken. Heart trouble."

Kellyn held the frame next to his face again. "That's where you get those gorgeous eyes. I'm sorry you lost her, Pace."

He took the frame from her and put it in its place. He stroked her cheek, then sat on the edge of the bed. "I don't have a lot of girls in my room."

She turned her head to the side and cut her eyes at him. "What are you getting at, Samson?"

"I just…" He felt like an idiot. "You probably don't care, but I usually take girls to their place, not here."

"You don't like to be impolite and tell them to go when you're done with them?"

Heat spread up his neck into his face. "Seems

kind of rude to do that when I can just sneak out after they fall asleep in their own bed."

"*That's* not rude at all."

"It saves a lot of awkward goodbyes, and I'll call you later lies."

"Practical." She let out a breath. "Why am I here?"

"Because the bathroom wasn't very romantic."

She raised an eyebrow. "I thought we needed some new bathroom memories."

The truth was something he'd never admit. A woman had never gotten him so hot with her kisses, and when he felt the heat between her legs, he nearly lost it. He would have if Cobie and Indi hadn't interrupted. It was embarrassing, and he didn't want Kellyn to know the affect she had on him. He needed to remain in control and aloof.

He blinked and looked up to see her watching him. "Oh, right, we definitely need new bathroom memories, especially when we get back to your place. Let's go."

* * *

For the second time that night, Kellyn saw Pace struggle internally with something and then shut down. The openness was gone and replaced by the Pace he showed to the world.

He stood at the bedroom door and held it open for her. If he thought he was going to her house, so he could sneak out after sex, he was mistaken. But she didn't want to be hurtful. He was clearly trying to decide who he wanted to be when he was with her.

"You know what, Pace?" She put her hand on

her stomach. "I don't feel so well. I'm just gonna go home and rest."

"Oh, um, okay." His forehead wrinkled. "I'll walk you out."

She walked into the living room. "Goodnight, you guys."

"Kellyn, wait." Indi got off of the sofa where Cobie had been laying with his head in her lap. "Are you okay? He wasn't mean to you, was he?"

"No, he wasn't." *Not exactly.* "Look guys, I appreciate you looking out for me, but you can't keep interfering with what Pace and I have going. I'm a big girl."

Kellyn had planned to tell Pace not to walk her out before Indi stopped her at the door. Then, it seemed better to let Pace go through the motions of pretending he cared. It might give him a boost in the eyes of their friends.

Her shoulders dropped once she was clear of the prying eyes. Trying to figure out how she had gone from concerned, to hot and bothered, to friends, to nothing at all was giving her a headache. Absentmindedly, she rubbed her forehead with her fingertips.

"I thought it was your stomach," Pace said from behind her.

"Now, it's my head." She unlocked her car, and he got the door for her.

They'd never even had sex, so she couldn't understand why she felt rejected.

"Why did you lie?" he asked.

"About what?"

"Your stomach…and you told them I didn't

hurt you, but that's a lie. I saw it on your face."

"You're moody, Pace." *Pot...kettle.* "Maybe we still need to recover from last night." She tried to close the car door, but he stopped her.

"Wait, why did you stand up for me? For us?"

"I don't know, Pace. This feels...a little too serious. Flings are supposed to be fun. I'm not sure we're gonna work."

"What? No, I can't let you go, Kellyn. I actually like you. Give me chance. Scoot over."

"What?"

"Scoot over, I'm driving. I'm taking you home to take care of you, since you're sick." He sat on her lap and tried to swing his legs under the steering wheel, but they didn't fit.

Her laughter bubble burst again, and she struggled to breathe while she pushed him toward the door. "Claustrophobic, remember?"

"Oh, crap. I'm sorry." He shot out of the car like lightning.

She shook her head at him and climbed over the center console and into the passenger seat of her Civic, bumping her head three times in the process. If she didn't have a headache before, she would very soon.

"Pace—"

"Uh-uh, don't want to hear it." He turned up the radio and start singing along with Toby Keith.

Kellyn couldn't help but laugh at how ridiculous he sounded—both the singing and the new attitude. She reached over and held the hand resting on his knee, then turned to look out of the window. She smiled when he raised her hand to his lips and kissed it, causing her heart to flutter in her chest.

She'd been trying to protect herself when she attempted to break it off with him. Somehow, she knew it would be impossible not to fall for him. It had already begun.

Chapter Ten

Pace carried Kellyn up the stairs to her room, even though she protested. He didn't think she was really sick, maybe sick of his games. He decided to be real with her, all the way.

He laid her on the bed. "What can I get you? Pepto? Tylenol? Ice pack?"

"Tylenol's under the sink. I could get it myself, but I sense that's not gonna happen."

"Smart girl." He grabbed a bottle of water from the fridge.

On his way back upstairs, the door opened, and the other roommate came in with her back to him.

"Hi, Heather," he said. He'd never met her, but knew her name.

She didn't acknowledge him, so he continued on his way.

"Is Heather deaf or something? Because if not, she was just rude to me."

"Hearing impaired," Kellyn explained.

Pace covered his mouth with his hand, shocked at his own insensitivity to a disability. "I didn't know."

"She has hearing aids, reads lips, knows sign language, and can talk. Most of the time, you can't even tell when she speaks."

His lips stretched as soon as the thought entered his brain. "So if we make a lot of noise, she won't be able to hear us?"

"Why would we make a lot of noise?"

"You know, that's what girlfriends and boyfriends do."

Her laugh was dry. "We're still playing at that, are we?" She swallowed a couple of Tylenol and chased them with water.

"As soon as that X kicks in, we're gonna make some noise."

Her jaw dropped and her eyes widened. "You did not." She opened the pill bottle and let out a laugh. "Good one."

The laugh was what he was going for. *A fling was supposed to be fun.* Her earlier words had hit him like a jab. He planned to deliver and have fun doing it.

"Have you ever done it?" he asked.

"X? No, I'm a fraidy-cat when it comes to illegal substances."

"I don't recommend it." He laid on the bed next to her. "Do you have music?"

She rolled over and put her phone on the docking station next to the bed. Luke Bryan's voice flowed from the speakers.

Pace rolled onto his side to face her and played

with her hair.

"I think you should kiss me, so we can get this over with. You do have protection, don't you?" She raised an eyebrow.

He reached to pat his back pocket. "Oh hell, I left in such a hurry, I don't have my wallet, keys, or phone. Why don't you run down to the store and get some, baby?"

"Kiss my ass and don't call me baby." She swatted at him.

"I'm only playing. There's no rush, except you just want *to get it over with*, like it's a chore."

"I was only playing about that. I meant the awkwardness."

"I know you're sexually frustrated." He crawled on top of her. "I can help you without needing a condom to do it."

"Help me? Okay, help me all you want, but don't start begging to put it in when you want to be inside me so bad you can't stand it."

He flopped onto his back and growled. "You're right. Have you been in that situation before?"

"Have you?"

"No, but I know I'll want to keep going. You should've taken those condoms I tried to give you at the beach."

"The next time you offer me condoms, I'll take them." She grinned.

He rolled back onto his side. "Well, since we can't have sex, we could just go to sleep, again."

"Or, I could go to the store—"

"No way, I won't have you telling stories on me like you do Jacobs."

"You're one of three or four people who've ever heard that story." She rolled onto her side and propped her hand on her hip.

"You're sassy even when you're lying down." He leaned in and kissed her.

His body reacted to her taste and her heat. Without thinking, his hand moved to her hip. Her hand rested on his chest before it slid up to his neck. He rolled her onto her back and scooted closer, crossing his leg over hers and pressing himself into her hip.

God, he wanted her. "Come on. We're going back to my place."

"I could ask Heather if she has any or…" She paused and bit her lower lip. "I can't believe I'm going to even suggest this. No, I'm not. Sorry, I'll go ask Heather."

He waited on the end of the bed, and when she came back empty handed, he said, "Come home with me."

"We're bed hopping tonight, aren't we?"

"Musical beds. Wanna play?"

* * *

Kellyn chewed her cheek as she drove them back to Pace's apartment. She should just drop him and run, but that's not what she wanted. It was time to tell her brain to shut the hell up, so she could live a little.

"What were you going to suggest earlier?" Pace's voice made her tingle.

"I don't want to say. I still need to protect myself."

"From what?"

"STDs. My boyfriend has a bad reputation for laying pipe around town."

"You're on the pill?"

She nodded.

"I've never had unprotected sex, but I'm glad you're smart enough to stay safe."

"And considering Indi and Cobie..." She shook her head.

"I agree we should be extra careful. Kinda kills the libido to think about them, doesn't it?"

They had to knock for a few minutes, and Kellyn texted Indi before Cobie let them in.

"Sorry, man, forgot my keys," Pace said.

"We were getting ready for bed," Cobie said. "Y'all want to do breakfast in the morning?"

"Yeah," Pace said. "Knock on our door when you get up."

Kellyn detoured to the bathroom before joining Pace in his room. Music played and he was lying back on the bed with his hands behind his head, watching her with a big grin. A whole sleeve of condoms rested on her pillow.

She closed the door and locked it. "You look like a kid in a candy store."

"I do feel like I'm about to get a treat. Why shouldn't I be happy?"

"Oh, I think you should. We both should."

"Well, come on over here, Red."

Her heart rate had begun to increase the closer they got to the apartment, and now it was nearing the aerobic threshold. She was sure she'd go anaerobic or die during sex.

He got off the bed and came to her. "Take a

deep breath. If you're nervous, we can wait."

She tried to say something, but her mouth was dry, so all she could muster was a nervous laugh.

He pulled her to the bed. "Lie down. I'll give you a back rub."

"You don't have—"

"I insist. It'll help me relax too. I don't know why I'm so tense. When we're just hanging out, I'm very comfortable with you, but when we lock the door, I get…flustered."

She laughed and lay down on her stomach. He straddled her butt, and eight strong fingers and two thumbs sank into the muscles of her shoulders. His hands were like magic, and her eyes started getting heavy.

They popped open when his lips brushed the back of her neck, causing her skin to tighten and a moan to escape her throat.

"Let's get this shirt off and I can use lotion." He tugged the bottom of her shirt and eased it up.

She raised up enough to get it over her chest then lay back down and let him slip it over arms. The lotion was cold, and she tensed and gasped.

"Sorry, that had the opposite effect than intended." His lips pressed against her neck again as he kept working the lotion.

"Wow, cold to hot in the blink of an eye. You're good."

"I think with this hair," he stroked it, "your pilot light is always on, Red."

He left a trail of hot kisses down her spine until he got to her bra. After a short pause, he kept moving down until he reached the waist band of her jeans. Without his asking, she lifted her hips, and he reached around to the button. His lips trailed the jeans all the way down to her ankles.

"Turn over for me," he said.

She did and propped on her elbows to see him standing at the end of the bed watching her. Since she'd become Pace's "girlfriend", she'd started wearing pretty matching bra and panty sets, knowing this moment would come.

"Are you gonna stare at me all night?"

"I could, but that's only fun for me." He crawled up the length of her body and rested on his elbows, sliding one leg between hers.

A little more hot kissing and caressing and she was ready for skin to skin contact. "Let's roll." She pushed against his chest and reversed their positions.

She moved from his lips to his neck and enjoyed the shudder of his body and the sharp intake of breath. Taking the hem of his t-shirt in her hands, she left his neck and moved to put her lips on his belly and kissed up his body as she pushed the shirt. He rocked his torso to help her get it up, then crunched up so she could pull it over his arms. She paused to appreciate his abs.

When the corners of his lips turned up, she claimed them again and let her fingertips explore the ridges of muscle along his torso. Kissing her way down to the button on his jeans, she paused to cut her eyes up at him. The serious face and hooded eyes melted into his heart-stopping grin.

"I can't wait to see who we have on the shorts tonight." She unbuttoned the pants and pulled them open. "Lips? Come on."

"I knew you'd hate them. Go ahead and take 'em off, so you don't have to look at them."

She did, and when she got to the end of the bed, she stood to observe.

"Are you gonna stare at me all night?" he asked.

"I would, but Russell the Love Muscle keeps waving at me to come say hello."

"Did you just name my Johnson? Because I kinda like it."

"I can see that." Her body shook with laughter.

He waited while she crawled back up to him. When she hesitated near Russell, he reached down and pulled her up and rolled them again, so he was on top.

He took his time removing her bra and exploring the parts of her he said he'd been dying to get his hands on. Mouth too. All she could do was arch her back and struggle to breathe.

He left a hot, wet trail down to her hips and looked up at her as he gripped each side of her panties. "These are very pretty, but they've got to go."

She smiled and lifted her hips until he got them past her butt. Then she lifted her legs to help him get them off. He tossed them across the room and lay back on his side next to her. While his fingers got to know her intimately, her hands were also on an adventure across the hard planes of his body until she cupped him in her palm.

He moaned and jerked, pushing into her hand. "I think it's time," he said.

"Past time." She reached to where he left the condoms on the pillow beside them.

She opened a package and rolled it on before she noticed the surprised look on his face. "You can do it next time."

He kissed her again. "I like that you did it. That can be your job from now on."

They spent another moment kissing as he moved into position. Holding himself up, he looked into her eyes and hesitated. She couldn't wait another second to have him, so she opened and guided him inside. His eyes rolled back just before hers, and the rest was a writhing, bucking, moaning, fingernail digging bliss out.

Chapter Eleven

Pace awoke when the sun streamed in through the slit in the curtains. He was behind Kellyn with his arms around her; a position he remembered from the beach trip. Except this time, they were both naked, and Russell was waking up to say hello.

He placed light kisses all along her neck and shoulder until she moaned and leaned into him. He'd never had morning sex before because he was always too busy making his escape. He had nowhere to go…and didn't plan to leave anyway.

With his arms around her, he let one roam up high and one down low until she was writhing against him. He could spend all day doing this, and he hoped she would agree to stay and play.

There was a knock at the door. "We're up," Cobie said.

"Okay," Pace said. "Kellyn, we could go to breakfast or stay here and have more fun."

"We can do both."

He heard the tear of the foil package and buried his face into her neck, smiling like a clown under the big top.

He held on as long as possible, but when it was time, he said, "Oh, my God, Kellyn."

She chuckled when he collapsed on top of her and wrapped him into a tight hug. "You've said that a lot in the last few hours."

"My new favorite phrase." He kissed her cheek next to her ear, and Cobie knocked on the door again.

"Did y'all go back to sleep?"

"No, almost ready," Kellyn called then whispered, "Where did you toss my panties last night?"

When they were up and dressed, he took her face in his hands and planted a kiss on her luscious red lips, which were redder and lusher than normal.

Over breakfast, Pace tried to conceal the thrill vibrating through his body and his heart. Soon, they were laughing and joking like normal with her eye rolls and his crassness.

"I'm glad you guys are getting along so well," Indi said.

"Me, get along with him?" Kellyn pointed in his direction.

He caught her finger and kissed the tip of it.

"Do you know where that finger's been?" she asked.

"Uh-huh, I do. It's been in naughty places," he whispered the last part close to her ear.

He watched the color rise in her cheeks, and he gave her a wink, stopping himself from touching her cheek. He moved his arm from around her and clenched his fists under the table to remind himself that affectionate touching in public would invite speculation. He knew he shouldn't care, but if something went wrong, he didn't want everyone to know he'd failed at the boyfriend thing.

Kellyn interrupted his thoughts when she covered his fist with her hand and whispered, "We're just having fun; don't over think it."

He took her hand in his and squeezed it. Then, the wedding and baby talk started. Pace tried to zone out, but he wanted to hear everything Kellyn had to say. The sound of her voice tickled his ears when he thought about the things she'd whispered to him in his bed.

"You got that, Pace man?" Cobie asked.

"Huh, what? I was somewhere else."

"We want to keep the pregnancy a secret from everyone at school until after the wedding. We need you and Kellyn to help."

* * *

The next several weeks passed quickly. Pace and Kellyn spent at least one night of the weekend with Indi and Cobie at a bar—Kellyn drinking Indi's drinks and Indi pretending to get drunk.

One night, Kellyn exited a bathroom stall to find Jessica Hart waiting for her.

"When he's done with you and dumps your ass and breaks your heart, I'm gonna laugh." Jessica's smug expression nearly pushed Kellyn's temper into the danger zone.

Kellyn took a deep breath and let it out while she washed her hands. "I'm sorry for you, Jessica. If you can take joy in someone's pain, you must be miserable."

Kellyn walked past her and out to where Pace waited for her. He looked behind her and immediately asked what Jessica wanted.

"She wants you."

"She can't have me because I'm all yours." He tipped her back with a kiss that made her panties smolder.

They'd made up rules for their fling, and as time passed, it got harder to abide by some of them. They wouldn't call it a relationship—although, boyfriend and girlfriend were used often—and they would never use the L-word. They could *like* things all day, but never the big L-word. Needless to say, they sang a lot of la-la-las at times.

"I la-la-like it when you touch me like that."

Another rule was no gifts, but Kellyn had an idea for something she wanted to make him for graduation. The word "Graduation" was supposed to make her happy, but it drained her joy because they agreed it would mark the end of their fling.

She held the small shells they'd picked up while walking the beach together over Spring Break. The contest had been to see who could find the smallest shell. Pace won and he'd kept his prize find.

Pace had basically moved in with her because they had more privacy without Indi and Cobie down the hall, and since Indi practically lived with Cobie, it seemed fair. Kellyn wasn't about to complain. She was having the time of her life.

They even tried cooking together at her house,

but since he'd distracted her with counter sex, she burned the chicken. He agreed to be in charge of meals from then on.

"You really should learn to cook. Grad…" He hesitated. "Graduation is around the corner, and you're gonna have to survive on your own."

"Uh-uh, I'm moving home with my folks. I won't be solely responsible for my meals for a while. Besides, I can cook salad, no problem."

He laughed and threw a carrot at her, which she dodged.

One Saturday afternoon, they were killing time in her bedroom, waiting on laundry. They were both breathing heavy when they heard a crack and a thud.

Pace froze and looked at her with wide eyes.

"I think we broke the bed." She giggled uncontrollably for a few seconds.

"I'm afraid to move. What if we go crashing down?" His eyes were wide.

"Let's get up and see." She pushed against his chest, but he didn't budge. "Come on, tough guy, on the count of three."

He rolled off the bed and she followed. They stood together, naked, and looked at the split wood of the side rail. The metal underneath was bent in the same area.

Pace grabbed his stomach and bent over, laughing. "I've never broken a bed before."

"My dad is gonna kill me."

He put an arm around her. "We'll fix it. He'll never know. I've got to get a picture of this."

"No." She picked up a pillow and held it in

front of her. "You know the rule; no cameras while we're naked."

"Okay, no pictures, but I will need Cobie's help to fix this."

"He's gonna tell everyone."

"We're keeping their secret; they can keep ours."

"Smart man, I knew I la-liked you for a reason."

With a wicked grin, he moved the pillow and backed her up against the wall. "You la-like me?"

She swallowed and nodded, hoping he wouldn't press the issue. Instead, he pressed her into the wall. It was one of the sexiest things she'd ever done, at first. When her arms began to fatigue from holding on to him, she lost the almost O and slumped against him.

He repositioned his arms, one under her butt and one around her upper back. "Hold on...just...a...little...Oh, my God, Kellyn."

His words, his arms, and the feel of him pulsing inside her got her where she needed to be, and she let out a ragged breath, signifying her release. When her feet were on the floor, he gave her a sloppy, wet kiss and licked the side of her face.

She scrunched her nose and wiped the spit off. "Would you stop doing that?"

"You know I think you're cute when you make that face." He placed a light kiss on the tip of her nose.

She'd never admit she would miss his slobber and a lot of other things.

Chapter Twelve

Graduation was nearing, and so was the end. Pace's chest hurt when he thought about it. He'd gone and fallen in love. But they had an agreement and plans to go their separate ways.

On more than one occasion, he'd stopped himself from asking her to move with him to Atlanta. They could live together, and she could find a teaching job there. He wasn't ready for marriage, but he wasn't ready to let her go either.

He constantly reminded himself to have fun and not let Kellyn see him get moody. She could read him well, and she would know what had him down, so he put on his smile and made jokes to keep her laughing and loving him. He knew she felt it too. They both corrected themselves from time to time to keep from saying it. Once, when he was sure she was asleep, he'd whispered it, testing the feel of the words on his lips.

Caps and gowns were ordered, and their

parents made arrangements to come into town the night before graduation. Pace was bummed because they lost a night. They'd agreed to spend Thursday night together and meet for a drink Friday afternoon before their parents arrived. The idea was it would be better to say goodbye outside the bedroom.

Pace sat at the bar, waiting on Kellyn and stood when she came in, forcing his smile in place.

"Sorry I'm late. My parents came early to surprise me. I told them I had to run an errand." She hugged him and took the seat next to his.

They sat facing each other, and he wanted to pull her seat closer, but he knew it'd be better to keep some distance.

"I'll keep this brief then." He looked down, surprised to feel pressure behind his eyes. He hadn't felt that pressure in a long time, but he promised himself, no tears. He prayed the same on her part. Her crying might undo his resolve.

He took her hands. "Kellyn, you made me a better person."

"No, I can't take credit when what happened was you showed me who you really are. That's all you." She freed one hand and placed it over his heart.

"Whoever is responsible, I can honestly say knowing you changed me for the better."

She dropped her head and squeezed her eyes shut, inhaling a shaky breath. She let it out slowly before she looked up with shiny eyes.

"I'm not gonna cry." She smiled. "You taught me a lot about myself too, about who I can be." She paused and reached for her purse. "You were right when you said you'd be unforgettable. In the spirit of that, I know we said no gifts, but I made you something to remember me by."

She reached into her bag and placed something in his hand. The bracelet blurred as his eyes stung again. He examined the inch wide strap of soft, brown leather with a ring of shells circling it.

"It should fit because I measured your wrist while you were sleeping. Also, I know you can't wear it at work with your suits, but tuck it away somewhere. You can pull it out sometimes and remember our *Spring Fling*."

He put it on and smiled. "Great minds and all." He pulled her gift out of his pocket.

He had the tiny shell they'd found at the beach put on a monofilament line and made into a necklace. He wasn't talented enough to do it himself, but a professor in the art department had been glad to help out.

She put her hand over her heart. "I love-like it a lot. Thank you. Will you put it on me?"

He moved to stand behind her barstool, and she lifted her hair for him. After he latched the necklace, he took her hair and smoothed it down her back. He put his lips on the top of her head, inhaling the familiar scent of strawberries and Kellyn one last time.

He put his hands on her shoulders. "I hope you have a happy life."

"Wait," she said as he started to pull away. "I came here for a drink. One shot." She put in her request, and he sat back down and faced her.

They each took a shot glass and held them up.

After staring at each other for a moment, Pace said, "To something beautiful."

"To someone beautiful." She clinked his glass, and they tossed them back.

They made faces at each other afterward until they were laughing.

"I've got to run, but I'll see you at the wedding." She stood and kissed his cheek then wiped the lip gloss off with her thumb.

He watched her go and ordered another shot. Everything from his eyes, down his throat, to his stomach burned. He wanted to go after her. He didn't want it to be over.

His phone beeped. It was his dad letting him know he'd arrived. Pace dropped some money on the bar and decided not to let go, yet.

* * *

The following week was crazy. Kellyn mourned in her down time, but with the crowds at graduation, her parents getting her moved home, and gearing up for Indi's wedding, there wasn't much time to think. Going to bed without Pace was the hardest part. There were also those little moments when things would happen she wanted to joke about and she'd turn to find him *not* by her side. More than once, she'd typed a text message to him and deleted it before she hit send.

It was for the best. They were going to move forward and have happy lives. Kellyn had to believe that. She wanted Pace to be happy with all of her heart. Sometimes, it was hard not to dwell on the fact Pace had ruined her for all other men. Even though they'd had a rough start, he would always be the standard by which she compared all others.

Her parents went with her to Hilton Head for Indi and Cobie's beach wedding. Indi had been home with her several times, and since Kellyn had told them about the baby, her parents wanted to show their support. She was selfishly glad to have them around as a distraction, even though there was only one person on her mind when her toes hit the sand. She touched the small shell resting against her chest.

The rehearsal was short and sweet, and Cobie's parents were having a low country boil at the beach house they'd rented. Afterward, the bachelor and bachelorette parties would commence.

Pace smiled at her across the crowd, and she winked as her heart thumped like the bass was turned up too loud. He turned away and so did she. He wasn't unfriendly, but kept his distance. She was glad because she was tempted to ask for one more night. But that would only lead to wanting another and another. She would never stop wanting to be with him.

Before they separated to go party, Cobie called Kellyn over. "This will be the last night you have to drink Indi's booze."

"One more drunken night, your kid's gonna owe me. I'm gonna get her wasted when she turns sixteen."

"He," Indi said. "We just found out. I don't know what I'm going to do with a boy since I have two sisters."

"You'll figure it out," Pace said. "And since it's a boy, Uncle Pace will get him wasted for all of those drinks his mama didn't have to consume."

"That settles it," Cobie said, "once he hits his teens, no visits to see Uncle Pace or Aunt Kellyn." Cobie turned his attention to Indi. "Be careful."

"You too, and no strippers."

"Don't say that, Indi," Kellyn said. "He might request the same of you, and you'll have to cover your eyes at the party."

"What?" Cobie said.

Pace put his arm around his friend's shoulders. "Kellyn's just messing with you, man."

"Bye, boys." Kellyn waved and they turned to go.

Chapter Thirteen

Kellyn almost fell on the floor, laughing at the surprised look on Indi's face when the *firemen* showed up and began stripping layers off. Kellyn drank Indi's shot and put a dent in her daiquiri, while the other girls were distracted by near naked man flesh.

The strippers were moving toward the bride, and Kellyn started to scoot away until one of the guys pulled her to her feet for some bumping and grinding. If they were two pieces of wood, they would have sparked from the rubbing. While Kellyn admitted he had a nice package, his wasn't the one she wanted.

Later, when Indi was pretending to be drunk and Kellyn was pretending not to be, they went to a bar. Indi's younger sister, Embry, who'd just finished her freshman year at a college in South Carolina, wouldn't shut up about how hot Pace was.

Kellyn felt Indi's eyes boring a hole into her to

get her reaction, but Kellyn kept her smile firmly in place.

"Listen, little sister," Indi said. "That boy has a bad reputation. Don't even think about hooking up with him."

The little sister looked to Kellyn. "You went to school with them. Is it true? Is he a bad boy?"

"Very bad." *But, oh so good.*

As if their words summoned him, Pace, Cobie and the rest of the bachelor party came into the bar. Indi stood and clapped her hands together like an excited little girl.

Her little sister slid into her vacant seat. "Tell me more. I might like bad boys."

Kellyn refused to have this conversation. She picked up Indi's drink and drained it before she looked around. "Speaking of bad boys, isn't that one of the firemen?"

"Where?" The girl was like an untrained dog on point, not sure where she should look.

"At the bar."

"Oh my God, he's coming over here." Embry bounced in her seat.

The faux fireman had a tray of drinks he placed on the table. "Ladies, I could use some help with these drinks."

Kellyn swore he was looking right at her, but she swayed in her seat, so it was probably wishful thinking. After Kellyn started on one of the fireman's drinks, he asked her to dance. A strong arm wrapped around her from behind.

"She's with me." Pace's words caused her heart to turn a complete flip in her chest.

* * *

When Pace first entered the bar, he'd located Kellyn. Right after, he saw the man eyeing her from the bar. When the man made his move, so did Pace.

"I think our respective parties might be over. Cobie is mad as hell about the strippers."

"Did you guys see strippers?" Kellyn asked.

"Yes."

"Then what the hell? Freaking double standards. Let me at him." Kellyn pulled away from him.

He'd seen her drunk a few times and was glad he was there to take care of her, so other assholes wouldn't try to take advantage.

"I have a proposition. Me, you, blankets, beach, sunrise. Let's end it the same way it began."

"How am I s'pposed to say no to that?" She hiccupped.

"You're not."

"Okay." She shrugged and fought a smile. When she swayed, he placed an arm around her waist to steady her.

He helped her out of the bar, and they walked to the hotel room he was sharing with his dad. "Wait here." He propped her against the wall.

He grabbed a couple of blankets and told his dad not to wait up.

Kellyn seemed more alert as they walked down the beach to find a semi-private spot near the dunes. She helped him spread a blanket, and he put the extra one in a corner to snuggle under later.

The night sky was clear, dark, and twinkling with thousands of stars. The air was heavy with salt and the woman in his arms was the woman of his dreams. They didn't talk, but they made love and held onto each other like it was the last time.

The sound of a bird overhead woke him, and he pulled Kellyn closer, cursing the lightening sky. When the sun peaked over the horizon, he shook her. "Here it is, Red."

They sat up to watch the day begin. From this location and time of year, it was bigger, brighter, and hotter than the first sunrise they'd shared, which was an apt metaphor for how their fling had turned into something bigger than either of them had expected.

"Perfect." Her voice was a whisper.

Her head was leaning on his chest, so he simply dropped his chin and kissed her hair.

Once the sun was fully risen, they folded the blankets and walked back to the hotel.

"I'll grab my keys and drive you—"

"No need, we're here too."

The elevator door opened on his floor, and he hesitated, unsure if he should see her to her room.

"I'll see you out there in a little while." She gave him a little push. "Don't worry about walking me to my room. My dad will be up and might not be thrilled to meet the man who kept his little girl out all night."

"Little girl my ass." He kissed her cheek and stepped off the elevator.

He didn't see her again until she was walking down the aisle, doing her bridesmaid duty. His lips stretched from New York to San Francisco at the sight of her. She was gorgeous in a teal dress and bare feet. When she caught his eye, her smile grew wider, and she dropped her gaze while her cheeks turned a pretty shade of pink.

He found her at the reception and hugged her. "We're out of here. My dad needs to get back."

"Okay."

"This must be Pace." The man next to her extended his hand. "John Crenshaw, I've seen your pictures on Facebook."

"This is my dad. He cyber stalks me," Kellyn said.

"And who do have we here?" Pace's dad approached.

"Dad, this is Kellyn."

To his horror, his dad hugged her. "It's nice to meet you at last. I've heard so much about you since the day we spoke on the phone. I told Pace he should take you out, but he insisted you were just friends."

Kellyn's dad introduced himself and said, "I thought they were dating until Kellyn said otherwise. I guess being the best friends of Indi and Cobie forced them to become close friends too."

They had no idea how close.

Chapter Fourteen

It was a hot day in early August when Kellyn's dad yelled the telephone was for her. It was strange to talk on the house phone when she almost always used her cell.

"Miss Crenshaw, this is Sadie Williams. I'm the headmistress at the Academy in Atlanta. Your former sorority sister, Tessa, teaches here and recommended you for a teaching position at our school."

Relief and excitement coursed through her. Things were quiet on the job front, and she had thought she might have to start waiting tables. Also, Pace was in Atlanta. The thought made her both happy and hesitant. She was dying to see him, but what if he didn't want anything to do with her?

The headmistress was still speaking, so Kellyn reigned in her runaway thoughts and focused on the conversation, making arrangements with the headmistress for a formal interview.

"Tessa asked me to tell you she needs a roommate, in the event everything works out like we hope it will," the headmistress said.

After exchanging closing pleasantries, Kellyn hung up, danced around the kitchen, screamed, and yipped until her parents came in from the backyard. She shared her good news, and her parents were equally thrilled because so far, all of the teachers in their school system were returning for another year, which left no openings for Kellyn.

The next person she wanted to tell was Pace, but she stopped herself before she hit send. They hadn't spoken or seen each other since the wedding in June. He was moving on with his life, and he didn't need her slowing him down. If she got the job, then she'd contact him.

* * *

The call she was waiting for came early on a Friday. Her mom was out of town, but she ran to tell her dad, who was about to go feed the catfish at the pond.

"Looks like we'll be moving you to Atlanta. I'm happy for you, baby. Hey, doesn't your friend Pace live there?"

"Yeah, I guess I should call him, but I'm sure he already has a ton of friends."

"Come with me and think about it."

She slid onto the seat of the golf cart her dad used to get around their rural property. At the pond, he sent her to turn on the water hose on the other side. She stopped behind a tree and pulled out her phone. Not taking time to think, she called Pace.

"Hello," a squeaky female voice answered.

"I must have the wrong number."

"Um, it says you are Kellyn. This is Pace's phone. He can't talk 'cause he's in the shower."

Icy fingers gripped her heart and she debated hanging up. "Okay—"

"This is a cool picture on the phone. It's like a shadowy figure with their head on fire. Like an angel. Do you want me to tell Pace to call you?"

"No, thanks. I made a mistake and dialed the wrong person in my contact list."

"Okay, I won't tell him, especially 'cause he probably doesn't want me answering his phone. I have to go. He's waiting for me in the shower. Bye."

Kellyn sank to her knees and struggled to breathe. She told herself to stop being ridiculous. They'd shared something special once, but it was over. Somehow, knowing he'd moved on killed the tiny hope inside that she'd ever meant anything to him. She vowed not to think about him every day and to concentrate on her plans to make a new life for herself in an exciting place.

* * *

Atlanta turned out to be different than she expected. She loved her job and co-workers, but she'd counted on Tessa to take her out and introduce her to people like she had freshman year. Since Tessa was newly involved with a man, her free time was spent with him.

One of the teachers at her school told Kellyn about a round-robin tennis social. Kellyn had never played tennis, but she borrowed Tessa's racquet and showed up. She was terrible at it, but she had fun and met a few people, including Brice Baldwin.

The name reminded her of Pace, but that was where the similarities stopped. Brice was over forty with long dark hair he wore pulled back into a ponytail. He was thin with sinewy muscles, but he looked good for his age. His wise cracks and her quick retorts made them instant friends.

Kellyn wasn't interested in dating him, but he asked her to hang out and have drinks, and she wanted friends so she agreed. They'd get together to hit tennis balls or sit by the pool at her apartment complex.

"I have someone I want you to meet," he said one day by the pool.

"Okay, what's the catch?"

"No catch. You're a sweet girl, and he's recently finished school and needs a good woman."

She laughed. "Is he cute?"

"You'll have to be the judge of that. I tell you what, let's go meet a few of my friends for a drink later. He'll be there, but I won't tell you who he is until afterward, so I can get your reaction and his. It may not work out, but it might be worth a shot."

Kellyn picked out one of the guys she thought was cute. His name was Vic, and they went out a few times, but she'd forced herself to go because he wasn't Pace.

* * *

Pace helped Lindsay, a busty blonde, into his Porsche. His dad had given him the car for graduation, and women loved it more than they did him. Not that he dated very much. He'd sulked over Kellyn for a long time before his co-worker took him bar hopping. Once back in the saddle, he was almost his old self again.

It was actually easier than college because he had no remorse about leaving after sex with a woman who would give it away to a man she'd just met. He had no respect for any of them. Every woman left him in a darker place than the one before. He knew what he wanted, but he wouldn't let his mind go there, not after he'd missed her every day and she'd dropped off the radar. He was sure it was to avoid him. Still, little things made him think of her, and every time he saw a redhead, his heart skipped a beat.

"I hope you like sushi." He opened the door to the restaurant for the blonde.

He ignored the hostess when the back of a woman with long red hair caught his eye. When he heard her laugh, his heart stopped.

"We'll sit at the sushi bar." He walked past the hostess, ignored his date, and took the empty seat next to the redhead, bumping her with his elbow. "I'm sorry, miss."

When she turned to face him, her smile faltered and then returned, but it wasn't the real thing. "Fancy seeing you here."

"You two know each other?" the prick with his arm around her chair asked.

At Kellyn's nod, the guy said, "That's so weird. We were just talking about it being a small world." He started humming *It's a Small World*.

"Don't do that," Kellyn said to her date, and he stopped.

"Kellyn and I went to college together. She can

111

be bossy; it's the teacher in her," Pace said to her date. "I'm surprised to run into you here in Atlanta. I would've thought I'd get a phone call at least."

"Hi, I'm Lindsay." Pace's date reached her hand out to Kellyn.

Kellyn looked at it a second too long before she shook it.

Everyone was introduced, and Pace ordered sake for them all to share.

"So, how long are you in town? Were you going to call me?"

"Man, you two *are* out of touch," Vic said. "Kellyn lives here now and teaches at… What's the name of your school?"

Kellyn answered and then Pace asked, "How did you two meet?"

"She met my buddy Brice at a tennis thing, and he introduced us."

"I play tennis," Lindsay said. "Flight one, what flight are you on, Kelly?"

Pace corrected her on the name, and Vic said, "I don't think they'll let her on a team. Brice says she's terrible."

Kellyn put her hand on her hip. "I'm getting better now that I've been taking lessons though. Oh gosh, there's my tennis coach walking in the door."

"Oh, my God." Lindsay watched the door. "Walt is your tennis coach?"

"Yeah, he's nice, just got engaged."

"Shut up!" She turned back. "I used to date him."

"Maybe I misunderstood." Kellyn shrugged.

"Kellyn, hi." The tennis coach approached.

"Sorry to interrupt your supper, but I wanted to introduce you to my fiancée."

Kellyn turned in her chair and spoke to the woman, but not with her mouth. Her hands were moving ninety to nothing as she communicated with Walt's fiancée.

Pace felt his jaw fall open. He knew she could sign a little, but he thought it was to talk to her roommate.

"I knew you two would be friends," Walt said also signing. "We'll leave you to it, and I'll speak to you soon, doll." He kissed Kellyn's cheek and so did his fiancée.

"What the hell, Red? When did you become proficient in sign language?"

She shrugged. "I started learning from a friend when I was young. It's one of the languages I teach at the Academy."

"One of the... What? Who are you?" Pace asked.

"You've seen me sign before—"

"But I had no idea you were qualified to teach." He'd thought they were just making up sign language in their private time together.

"You do know about my Spanish fluency." She poured another sake.

"From when you used to order at the Mexican restaurant? I thought you could just say the food items."

Vic interjected. "That's why you spent the summer in Spain?"

"You spent the summer in Spain? Dammit Kellyn, you don't tell me anything."

"Calm down, Pace." She leaned closer to speak in a low voice. "You're making your date uncomfortable."

"I'm sorry, Laura—"

"Lindsay." Both Lindsay and Kellyn corrected him.

"I'm sorry, Lindsay. It's just that Kellyn and I were very close four months ago, and I feel as if I'm sitting beside a stranger right now."

"My mom took me to Spain as a graduation present. She has friends there from when she studied abroad. I took a break from technology while I was away. No computers. No cell phones. It was the second hardest thing I've ever done."

"What was the first?" Vic asked.

She looked down at her plate. "Watching someone I cared about walk away from me."

Pace moved to put his arm around her, but caught himself in time to pull it back and clench his fist.

"Sorry." Vic rubbed her back. "I shouldn't have asked." He waited a beat. "So, are you going to go to that costume party with me next weekend?"

"I'm going to a costume party next weekend, too," Lindsay chirped.

Their dates exchanged enough information to find out it was the same party, and Lindsay asked Pace to go with her. If Kellyn was going with Vic, he wanted to be there, so he said yes.

He tried to turn his attention to his date, but with Kellyn inches away, he couldn't focus on anyone but her and how much he wanted her, even though she hadn't called him.

When he dropped Lindsay off and declined her offer to go in for a night cap, he got into his car and texted Kellyn.

Why didn't you call me???

Chapter Fifteen

Kellyn put on her seventies mini dress and boots to complete her Priscilla Presley outfit. She'd agreed to the costume because all she had to do was part her hair in the middle and poof it up a little. Vic loved music and Elvis in particular.

She was trying to like Vic, but she couldn't stop thinking about Pace. She'd almost called him, but remembered their agreement. The fling was over. And he hadn't called her, but then she'd made it nearly impossible for him to.

Vic guided her inside the house with his hand on her lower back. The porch was crowded with guests dressed in hot costumes, enjoying the cool October night air. Inside the house, the skimpy costume wearers were trying to stay warm.

She wasn't excited about seeing Pace with Lindsay, but she pasted a smile on her face and looked for the adult beverages. She needed a drink because the Elvis impersonating was already getting old.

Vic had serenaded her on the ride over, and while she liked Elvis music, it was hard to be charmed by her date singing ballads like "It's Now or Never" and "Are You Lonesome Tonight." He might as well come out and ask, "Am I gonna get laid?"

Kellyn wasn't interested in sex with Vic, but maybe she needed to try someone new to get over Pace. Her heart had betrayed her by falling for Pace and her body did the same when she laid eyes on him. He was dressed as Danny Zuko from *Grease,* and he was smokin' hot. It was hard to miss Lindsay dressed as vixen Sandy because she was draped over his arm. They were by the keg, so of course, that's where Vic steered her.

"Can I get you a drink, Miss Presley?" Pace asked.

"Yes, thank you." She looked around the room.

"You look so good as Elvis." Lindsay/Sandy rubbed her hand down Vic's arm. "Like a hunk of burning love."

Vic tucked his thumbs into his sparkly belt and curled his lip. "Thank you. Thank you very much."

"Take our picture." Lindsay gave Kellyn her phone and put her arm around Vic.

It didn't escape Kellyn's notice that Lindsay hadn't complimented her, only her date. She felt plain. She didn't remember vixen Sandy having so much cleavage. Kellyn barely aimed before she snapped the photo and handed the phone back.

"Careful, Priscilla. I think I see your claws

coming out." Pace/Danny handed her a red Solo cup of beer. "I suppose it would be hard to be the wife of the king and see the ladies wanting him all the time." He winked.

She smiled at Pace's words, but then cringed as she watched Vic do a song and dance number, which actually garnered a lot of female attention.

"You're making that funny face I like so much." His lips were close to her ear, and her pilot light flared.

Her face was hot. "Sorry."

"You changed your number." He sipped his drink.

"I had a little incident with my phone before I moved here." She didn't have to tell him she'd chucked it in the catfish pond after a girl answered when she'd called him.

"I went to your school, but I couldn't get past security."

She turned her head to look at him. "Why?"

"Pace, I've got to tell you something." Lindsay stepped between them and whispered in Pace's ear.

Kellyn looked the other way because Pace was staring at her over Lindsay's shoulder. She fidgeted and moved a step away.

When Lindsay left, Pace moved closer and leaned against the wall next to her. "What would happen if Priscilla and Danny had an affair?"

She'd been about to take a sip of beer, but his words surprised her so much, the drink spilled down the front of her dress. They were just outside the kitchen, so he took her hand and pulled her inside and grabbed a roll of paper towels. He tore off a few sheets, wadded them up, and started wiping her chest.

"There you are."

Kellyn jumped at Vic's voice and Pace's hand froze. She took the paper towels from him, not wanting to think about how it looked. "Had a little accident."

Vic's lip curled, but not because of who he was imitating. "You're a mess, and we haven't even gotten our picture taken yet."

Kellyn figured he'd stopped just short of saying she would make him look bad.

Lindsay stepped around them and hugged Pace's arm, pressing her boobs into him. "She can pose like this, and no one will be able to tell."

"We'll wait until it dries," Vic said. "I don't want you to get me wet."

You're never gonna get me wet at this rate.

Kellyn's face grew warmer when Pace smirked at her. He must've read her thoughts. His grin made her sweat. It could have been the polyester, but she knew better. He caused the kind of slow burn that could consume a woman. Lindsay was so lucky.

"Hey, the guys are here." Vic took off toward the front room, and Kellyn followed.

If Brice was there, she'd have someone to talk to, and he'd make sure she had fun, like Indi used to do. She also needed to put distance between her and Pace before she acted on her physical urges. Pace was playing with her, and she couldn't fall for it again.

She knew most of the guys and said hello, even got a few hugs, but Brice was not among them. She slipped out onto the porch for some fresh air and found a quiet set of stairs around the corner from where the band played.

Sitting there, she plotted her departure.

* * *

Pace looked around for Kellyn. When he couldn't find her inside, he went out and bumped into a fraternity brother on the porch.

After exchanging hellos, Vance asked, "Are you still seeing Kellyn?"

Pace wanted to say yes and she was off limits, but he surprised himself with what he did say. "I wish."

"Really? Cause I swore I just saw her. I was gonna grab a drink and go look for her."

"Yeah, she's here. Which way did she go?"

He pointed, and Pace tried not to run.

His heart thumped in his chest as he sat on the step next to her. "You didn't answer my question about the affair."

"You mean here, at the party?" She twirled the end of her hair. "Or later?"

"Does it matter?"

"I might need to divorce the king first." Kellyn hadn't looked at him yet.

He took her hand and held it to his chest. "Why didn't you call me?"

"I did, but when your new woman answered, I realized you'd moved on and I needed to too."

His jaw unhinged. "What woman?"

"Doesn't matter. We had our time." She pulled her hand away from him and stood.

He followed and stopped her. "No, Kellyn. I

can't let you—" He turned his head toward a sound at the back of the house. "Do you hear that?"

He pulled her arm, and she followed, bumping into him when he stopped abruptly. He put his arm around her and pulled her forward, so she could see what he saw. There was couple getting it on against the back wall of the house.

The king's jumpsuit and bedazzled belt was around his ankles, and he was balls deep in a certain vixen. The leather pants and bustier on the ground would've been enough to give her away, but the six inch platforms dangling from her feet and the shrill voice encouraging her lover to do her harder was confirmation.

Kellyn tensed under his arm. "I guess I need to find another ride home."

"Not before I get you that divorce." He tugged her arm and raised his voice. "Excuse me."

Vic froze. Lindsay screamed. Pace smiled when he heard his brother behind him. "Now that's something you don't see every day."

Vic scrambled to get his suit up, and Lindsay hid behind him, clutching her clothes to her chest.

"Vic, what the hell, man?"

Pace watched as an older guy with a Dracula cape and long hair put his arm around Kellyn.

"It wasn't my fault, man." Vic moved away, leaving Lindsay exposed. "She came on to me. I'm sorry, Kellyn, but if you'd been a sure thing, I wouldn't have done it."

Pace's body reacted outside of his control, and his fist landed on the side of Vic's face, knocking his shades off and making him stagger back.

"Thanks, man. You saved me from having to do that." Dracula extended his hand. "I'm Brice."

Pace shook off the pain in his knuckles and gripped the man's hand. "How do you know Kellyn?"

"I'm the idiot who introduced her to Vic. Guess I should've kept you for myself, kid." Brice kissed the top of Kellyn's head.

Pace clenched his fists again, and Vance put a hand on his shoulder. "Someone needs to help the nekkid gal."

"Don't look at me," Pace said. "She used to be my date."

"Pace." The whiny voice made him twitch.

"I'll take you home, Red." Brice turned Kellyn away from the scene of the crime.

"I'll take her." Pace took Kellyn's hand. "And I'm the only one who calls her Red."

Kellyn dug her heels in. "It's okay, Pace. Really. Brice is a friend."

Pace turned to face her. "I need to talk to you."

Kellyn bit her lip. "I think we've said everything."

His hands ran down her arms, and he took her hands. "I have more to say. Please hear me out."

"Let me talk to Brice a minute. I'll meet you on the front stairs."

Pace waited for what seemed like forever, while he chatted with Vance. He let out a long breath when he saw Kellyn round the corner of the porch with her friend. Pace ground his teeth.

Lindsay, finally dressed, stepped out of the front door and spotted Kellyn. "You bitch." She slung her beer.

The liquid soaked the front of Kellyn's dress and splashed onto her face and hair. She licked her lips, tasting the beer, before her lips turned into a sardonic smile. There was no sweetness in her expression, and that could only mean one thing.

She lunged.

Pace caught her around the waist and moved her away a few feet, swinging her off the ground. "Not worth it, Red." He set her down, smoothed her hair, and wiped her face. "Are you okay?"

She looked down at the beer dripping off her dress as tears filled her eyes. "A little wet and not in the good way."

He grinned as he took her hand. "Come on. I live close by. We'll get you cleaned up."

He opened the car door and she asked, "Who's car?"

"Mine." He explained how he'd gotten it.

"I don't want to damage it or anything."

"You won't. Get in."

Pace enjoyed watching her struggle to keep the mini dress covering her essentials as she settled into the low seat. When she looked up to see him watching, he licked his lips.

He drove them to the townhouse he'd recently purchased. After giving her a quick tour, he said, "Jump in the shower, and I'll find you something to wear."

He got clothes and leaned against the bathroom door, listening to the water run. He wanted to join her, but they weren't the couple they once were. He hoped they could be again, without the limits this time.

He knocked and cracked the door. "Clothes." He set them down and went to the fridge.

He opened two beers and sat on the couch. When she came in wearing his t-shirt and boxers, he laughed at the familiar image of Papa Smurf and the words "Who's Your Papa?" The laughter died in his throat when he noticed she was braless and turned on. He shifted in his seat as his pants got uncomfortably tight.

She crossed her arms over her chest, so he got up and pulled her to the couch.

"You don't have to cover up with me. I'm sorry I made you uncomfortable, but it's obvious you aren't wearing a bra."

"It was wet."

"I'm sorry about all that."

She picked up her beer bottle. "You know how to pick 'em."

"I pick them, so I won't like them…all except for you."

"You still like me?"

His pulse thundered in his ears. "Kellyn, I'm in love with you."

She blushed, then kissed him. Her lips were right, perfect, hot…like their sunrise.

He broke the kiss. "Does this mean you love me too?"

"Do you have any idea how many times I had to bite my tongue, so I wouldn't say it out loud?"

"How many?"

"A thousand."

"Is that all? Mine was more like a million."

"Well, mine was…" She started to play verbal ping-pong, but stopped and stroked his cheek. "It doesn't matter because I love you, Pace Samson."

Epilogue

Within six months, Kellyn moved in. Within a year of that, Pace proposed. In the spring of the following year, they got married on the beach in Panama City where it all started. Indi and Cobie stood up for them, and their son was the ring bearer.

As Pace carried her over the threshold of their honeymoon suite, he said, "When we have a daughter, she is never dating or going to college or joining a sorority, and especially not going on any beach trips with rogue boys."

"I don't know, if you never let her out of your sight, she may not meet the love of her life like I did."

Pace laid her on the bed and lowered himself over her. "Who knew spring flings could turn into true love?"

ABOUT THE AUTHOR

Meda White is an award-winning author who writes sweet, sultry, and southern contemporary and new adult romance. Born with Georgia clay running through her veins, she continues to enjoy the Southern lifestyle with her husband, a very spoiled Collie, and a stray cat who adopted the family. When not writing, you might find her making music, shooting zombie targets, teaching yoga, or explaining the meaning of her unusual first name.

A Note to Readers

Dear Reader,

Thank you for reading *Spring Fling*. I hope you enjoyed Kellyn and Pace's love story. I had fun writing about Panama City Beach, Florida where I spent many beach weekends and spring breaks during my youth. If you're interested in the other Southern College Novellas, stay tuned for a sneak peek at *Fall Rush*.

If you have a moment to leave an honest review, I'd really appreciate it. Not only do reviews let authors know how they're doing, they help readers find new books.

I love to hear from readers. Please look for me on my Website, Facebook, Twitter, and my Dirt Road Darlings street team. If you sign up for my Newsletter, which contains bonus material and sometimes prizes, it'll make sure you never miss a new release.

Thank you, and best wishes for a lifetime of love and laughter.

Meda

Fall Rush

Embry Harris rushed in the door, late for her first real day of work. She tried to catch her breath while she apologized to the manager and tied an apron around her waist. She'd been through training and had shadowed a few experienced servers, but she was still nervous about waiting tables by herself. It seemed so simple when she watched others do it, but balancing a tray of food and drinks was no easy feat. The owner of the sports bar had taken a chance on her, and she didn't want to let him down.

It was so unfair she had to work for spending money her senior year of college. If only her parents would've let her transfer to another college closer to home, things would've been better financially and otherwise. They'd insisted she stick it out at the main campus for her last year. She'd offered to quit the sorority to cut back on expenses, but her mom had nearly had a conniption fit.

Embry was a legacy and her grandmother, mom, and both of her older sisters were sisters in the Greek sense of the word. Not only was she forbidden to quit, she was forced to live in the house, spending even more money her parents didn't have.

As the youngest of three girls, Embry was grateful there was any money left for her college expenses. Her parents had dipped into her education fund to pay for her sister's lavish wedding. Since Omni was marrying into money, they'd wanted to impress the groom's family. If only they'd had a simple beach wedding like her eldest sister Indi had had two years earlier, life would be easier. The truth was Indi's marriage to Cobie had changed Embry's life, and not in a good way.

If Embry could survive this year and graduate, she'd move far away from South Carolina and never look back, which was funny considering her naivety when she'd started college three years earlier. Her goals then were to get a degree and fall in love with a fraternity boy who would propose at graduation. That stupid little girl was long gone.

She shook those thoughts off as she filled her drink order and lifted the tray, careful not to tip it too far in any direction. She practically held her breath as she made her way to deliver the beverages. She set them down without dumping them on anyone.

The lady with mile-high hair sipped her soda. "This tastes like diet."

"Yes, ma'am, that's what you ordered."

"I changed my mind." She shuddered. "I thought you heard me."

"Okay, regular Coke. I'll be right back."

"And I need lemon for my tea." The balding man tapped his glass.

"I need a straw." The kid swung his head to get his too long bangs out of his eyes.

Embry reached in her pocket and pulled out

straws for everyone.

"I'll be right back with Coke and lemon." Embry smiled and strode away.

"Miss, can you get our waitress? We're ready to order," a lady called as she passed.

It was one of Embry's tables, so she stopped to take drink orders on her way to the other errand. It was a mistake because they ordered drinks, appetizers, and food, which overwhelmed Embry to the point she forgot the first table until they stopped her again.

She spent most of her shift apologizing to people, but never so profusely as when she knocked over an ice water into a man's lap while she was clearing away dishes. Pete, the owner, wasn't going to be in until later, and the manager eyed her like a hawk spying a field mouse, ready to pounce when she least expected. After cleaning up the mess, she checked on her tables before going to the newest table in her section. She'd rather sit in a fire ant bed than go to that table, but they were customers too.

She put on her biggest, fakest smile and approached. "Can I get you guys something to drink?"

"Tease-me-Embry, what are you doing working here? Being a tease wasn't paying the bills?"

"Just earning some spending money. What are you drinking, Chase?" He was the guy she tried to date her sophomore year. When they'd gotten hot and heavy, she'd panicked and run out on him. He started calling her that name when she'd been too embarrassed to return his calls afterward.

The table of fraternity brothers placed their

orders, each giving his own little dig in turn. She'd only frozen up on Chase, but to hear them tell it, she did it to every brother on campus. She'd stopped trying to date or have sex after that. Of course, they stopped asking her out too. Being a pariah was hell on a sorority girl's love life.

ALSO BY MEDA WHITE

Fall Rush
A Southern College Novella

Embry Harris is desperate to turn things around her senior year of college. She's determined to make more responsible choices and rid herself of the stigma plaguing her. But because of her job and the hot bartender who goads her into making impulsive decisions, it isn't going to be easy.

Stede Bennett's mission since returning from his overseas tour is to get his degree. The last thing he needs is a spoiled sorority girl distracting him. Being a Marine taught him many things, except how to handle a beautiful woman in constant need of saving.

Protecting Embry from the jerk threatening to ruin her reputation is how Stede begins to lose his heart. Being empowered by Stede's words is how Embry starts losing hers. If the schemer responsible for pushing them together gets his way, they could lose their chance for happiness.

Winter Formal
A Southern College Novella

Life is going according to plan for Sibba Douglas until she gets blackmailed. Her future dream of being a doctor is threatened unless she can help a spoiled fraternity boy do well on the MCAT.

Nash Lincoln knows he needs to settle down and focus on his studies, but academics have taken a back seat to social events and he's coasting by on little sleep and lots of pills. The distraction of a tutor he's admired from afar isn't helping matters.

Substance abuse leads to tragedy and draws Sibba and Nash closer together. But it may also be the thing that tears them apart.

Christmas Give

A Holiday Novella

Eva Walker returns home to Georgia for the first Christmas since her husband's death. She's missed her family, but is afraid the void left by her husband will make it unbearable.

Between losing his job as an NFL defensive back and losing his wife to the star quarterback, Adam "Mack" Riggs has had a rough year. Looking for a change of pace, he visits an old college friend for Christmas.

The attraction between Eva and Adam is instant, and so is the laughter. Enjoying life again feels so good for both of them. Simple Christmas wishes unite with a shared holiday tradition, putting them on a path toward healing and acceptance. A path that could lead to a future, if only their pasts would remain where they belong.

THE SOUTHLAND ROMANCE SERIES

Play With My Heart
A Southland Romance Book 1

Southern musician and closet geek Liz Baker enjoys her quiet life. While in Los Angeles helping her brother with a house project, the simple life gets complicated when British television actor Ian Clarke walks into the picture.

Ian enjoys his celebrity status in Hollywood and is determined nothing and no one will get in the way of his plans for success on the big screen. He never counted on meeting a woman like Liz, but she's the only one who can help him with a personal problem.

Forced into close quarters where priorities and cultures clash, an intense attraction catches them both by surprise. Secrets, old lovers and the paparazzi threaten their new dreams and a chance for love could be lost forever.

Play With My Heart **is the 2014 BTS Red Carpet Award Winner in Contemporary Romance**.

Dance With My Heart: A Southland Romance Book 2
Ride With My Heart: A Southland Romance Book 3
Fool With My Heart: A Southland Romance Book 4